The Ice Mountain

"If you tried very hard, you would make a reasonable figure skater, but not, I fear, ever in the top echelon. There is a branch of the sport you could take to the top . . . ice dancing. If you're interested, come and see me here, the day after tomorrow. Oh and Benjamin, Wednesday night or never— you only get the one chance."

Benjamin couldn't resist going to the rink to find out just what this man was on about. And he was certainly surprised to see Belinda Thomas from his class at school there as his possible partner! But, after he had taken a few twirls and swirls on the ice, Benjamin had to admit that there was something about ice dancing that he liked.

Soon, the pair of them were training hard three nights a week. They jogged every morning and cycled whenever they could in between. Admittedly, their skating was improving but that didn't do much for their school work and it didn't take long before their form teacher began to notice.

But teachers weren't Benjamin's only problem. For a start, his father thought that skating was only for cissies: he wanted his son to be a rugby player, but Benjamin couldn't risk getting an injury that would interrupt his training. And then he had to lie to his friends. After all, he couldn't tell them that there were no games or mucking around for him because he was training to be a namby-pamby skater, could he?

Morris, their trainer, had told Benjamin and Belinda from the start that to take ice dancing seriously meant hard work. Now it was beginning ~~to~~ ~~~~ ~~~~hat they had a moun~~~~ ~~~~ ~~~~ ~~~~ ~~~~ ~~~~nountain—and if th~~~~ ~~~~ ~~~~ ~~~~ ~~~~ ~~~~they got to the top .

The Ice Mountain

Nicholas Walker

Hippo Books
Scholastic Publications Limited
London

Scholastic Publications Ltd.,
10 Earlham Street, London WC2H 9RX, UK

Scholastic Inc.,
730 Broadway, New York, NY 10003, USA

Scholastic Tab Publications Ltd.,
123 Newkirk Road, Richmond Hill,
Ontario L4C 3G5, Canada

Ashton Scholastic Pty. Ltd.,
P O Box 579, Gosford, New South Wales,
Australia

Ashton Scholastic Ltd.,
165 Marua Road, Panmure, Auckland 6,
New Zealand

First published by Blackie and Son Limited, UK, 1986

Published in paperback by Scholastic Publications Ltd., 1988

Text copyright © Nicholas Walker, 1986

ISBN 0 590 70780 9

Made and printed by
Cox and Wyman Ltd., Reading, Berks

Typeset in Plantin by
AKM Associates (UK) Ltd
Ajmal House, Hayes Road, Southall, London

For Mu

Contents

1

Anyone for Coffee?

By 9 o'clock, Monday morning, one thousand nine hundred and twenty-two pupils of Summercourt Comprehensive had arrived at school. Of the eighty-nine missing, thirteen were going to be late, fifty-one were ill, two were abroad, nine were playing truant, two were at the dentist's, ten were on a day course at Stourbridge Art School, and one had got on the wrong train at New Street Station in Birmingham and was now hurtling towards London.

In a house just over two kilometres from the school the two thousand and eleventh pupil was still asleep, a broad smile on his face. By the bedside stood a Mickey Mouse alarm clock set for nine-fifteen.

At nine-thirty, just when the rest of the school were jamming into Assembly, Benjamin Trueman was emerging from his front door wheeling a bicycle and clutching an apple for breakfast.

Ten minutes later he dumped his bike in the bike sheds and peered anxiously around the door at the two prefects who were positioned at the library window for latecomers.

The prefects were busy playing cards and hardly noticed the fourth former with a crate of milk perched on his shoulder. Benjamin put the caretaker's milk down in the cloakrooms and crept past the packed hall and the empty staff room, where he borrowed a newspaper from the pile by the door.

By the time Monday's prolonged Assembly was over, he had marked himself present in the form register and was reading the *Daily Express* while finishing off a bottle of the caretaker's gold top.

Benjamin Trueman was hiding from the Maths master behind the huge form of Christopher Jenkins. Robert Stevens, Benjamin's best friend, was pretending to copy the Maths off the blackboard but in reality he was compiling a rugby team for Saturday's game. Rob, head of fourth year games, took his job seriously.

"I'm not going on the wing again," Benjamin whispered. "They all know me. Every time I make a move great giants fall on me."

"You're the fastest man in the team, you've got to go on the wing," Rob said definitely.

"Who's playing centre three-quarter? I want someone with muscles."

"Me of course. Don't panic, I'll keep them off you, then you can get all the glory as usual."

Mr Coup's voice cut across the room. "Are you listening, Trueman?" he demanded.

Benjamin jumped. "I think so, sir."

"You think so?"

"Yes, sir."

"You're an idiot, aren't you, Trueman?" Mr Coup said.

"Oh yes sir, a complete idiot," Benjamin agreed eagerly. "Mrs Hopkins says I'm not worth bothering with. She gave up trying to teach me French in the second year—sir."

"I know just how she feels," Mr Coup said wearily, "but unfortunately for you, I haven't yet given up trying."

"You haven't, sir?" Benjamin said, disappointed.

"No I haven't. Moreover, unlike French, Mathematics is not a subject you can drop at GCSE." He gestured at the board. "Now tell us all how you would go about solving these."

Benjamin glanced at the two equations on the blackboard.

"I'd multiply the second one by three then I'd add them together—sir." Benjamin gave Mr Coup a smile.

"There you are. That didn't hurt, did it?" Mr Coup said. "Oh, all right, dismiss," he said as the bell started to ring.

"You were lucky," Rob said.

"Not at all, if you'd bothered to do last night's homework, you'd have recognized a simultaneous equation too."

"I had far more important things to do than Maths homework," Rob said. "I was taking the lovely Cheryl bowling last night."

"Cheryl Peters? I didn't even know you knew her," Benjamin said.

"I didn't until yesterday morning, but she was on

the library desk and I suddenly found a strong desire to read."

"Oh," Benjamin muttered. He was envious of Rob's easy manner with girls. He changed the subject.

"I think I've worked out how to fiddle the new coffee machine," he said, "so if my theories are correct then I'll stand you a cup."

"That's very big of you," Rob laughed, "and if it doesn't work then I suppose I'll have to fork out, as you'll be broke as usual."

"It'll work," Benjamin said, "all it needs is a minor technical adjustment." Two girls pushed past them. He stepped back, bumped into a chair and fell over with a crash.

"Try and stay on your feet, Dizzy," Josey Law said. (Dizzy was Benjamin's nickname.)

"It's exhaustion," Belinda Thomas said, "all that work he's been doing for Coup." The two girls strolled off leaving Benjamin sitting on the floor, staring after them.

"Why don't you ask her out?" Rob said.

"Eh—who?" Benjamin said, scrambling to his feet.

"Who!" jeered Rob. "Belinda Thomas, that's who."

"Why don't you?" said Benjamin, avoiding the question.

"I have done—twice."

"And?"

Rob grinned. "There's always a third time—come on, break'll be over before I've got some coffee out of you."

They waited at the end of the queue for the coffee machine. At last the crowd cleared and Benjamin took a quick look round to make sure no one was watching.

"Now," he said, "I reckon that the coins must pass between two spring-loaded contacts about here." He gave the machine a hard bang. "Then the two contacts should touch each other and . . . ah!"

Rob stared in disbelief as a cup dropped down and started to fill.

"That was the minor technical adjustment, was it?" he asked. "You thumping it?"

"That was it." Benjamin handed Rob a cup. "My round I think." Another cup started to fill, Benjamin reached for it and raised it in a triumphant toast to Rob. Another cup dropped down.

"Oh dear," Benjamin said uneasily. Rob started to laugh. Benjamin banged the machine again. Still cups continued to fill. Benjamin now had two cups in either hand and was frantically trying to remove a fifth without spilling any. Rob was doubled up with laughter.

Benjamin gave up, dropped the cups and hammered with his fists on the machine.

"Stop it! Stop it!" he cried. He marched round the machine, banging it in various places. Rob grabbed his arm.

"Come on," he gasped.

"We can't just leave it," said Benjamin, "it'll take over the whole school."

"Come on," repeated Rob, dragging him away. Coffee was now pouring down the front of the machine on to the floor. They hurried off, Rob still shaking with laughter and Benjamin casting uneasy glances behind him as he went.

Benjamin was uneasy all day but finally he relaxed in Mrs Hopkins' French lesson, the last lesson of the day. It looked as though he'd got away with it. Nobody was going to bother about the coffee machine now.

Mrs Hopkins was their form teacher and she tended to leave him alone. Benjamin had never got along with French and as he was good at other subjects, she had reluctantly let him slide further and further behind.

Suddenly the door was flung open and Mr Grimshaw the Deputy Head stalked in. He gave Mrs Hopkins a cursory nod then turned to the form.

"Someone has vandalized the coffee machine," he snapped.

"Damn," Benjamin muttered.

"I want to know if anyone here had anything to do with it," Mr Grimshaw continued. There was complete silence.

"You're all quite sure are you?" he said. "If the person responsible comes from the fourth year then it's bound to be from this form. Four East and Four West were playing football and I personally made Four North work through the morning break."

No one stirred.

"Very well," he continued, "if I don't find the culprit then the whole school will suffer. The machine will be removed."

Benjamin stood up.

"Oh yes, I might have known," Mr Grimshaw said. "What on earth were you playing at, Trueman?"

"I only gave it a tap, sir, and it sort of stuck."

"I bet it did. Well, I hope for your sake that it doesn't cost much to repair."

"I don't think it will, sir," Benjamin said eagerly. "It's just that the spring contacts . . . "

"Trueman," Mr Grimshaw interrupted him.

"Yes, sir?"

"Be quiet!"

"Yes, sir."

"You can go into detention class for an hour this evening." As Benjamin opened his mouth, Mr Grimshaw added: "And if you say one more word it'll be two hours." He gathered his faded gown around him and strode out of the room just as the final bell began to ring.

"You got off lightly," Rob said.

"Oh Grimey's all right," Benjamin said. "It's a pity though, I was going to the rink. I'll have to go without tea now."

"Why not give it a miss?" Rob suggested. "Just this once."

"Oh, I don't know."

"It's an hour's ride each way as well, isn't it?"

"About that."

"You must be mad."

"Maybe," Benjamin said slinging his French books anyhow into his desk. "I'd better be getting along to the detention room." He pulled a face. "It's under Rawlings as well, I think."

"I suppose you want me to tell your dad for you?" Rob said.

"Yes, please."

"I'm good to you, it's out of my way you know."

"One good turn deserves another." Benjamin beamed at him. "I treated you to coffee, didn't I?"

2

Morris

That same evening, a man was standing in the Manager's office, looking out across the ice rink. He had been waiting for over an hour.

"I thought you said seven o'clock," the man said. "Are you sure he's coming?"

"He'll be here, he never misses," the Manager said. The man grunted, patience wasn't one of his virtues.

"That's him." The Manager pointed. The second man watched as Benjamin forced his way though the circle of beginners struggling round the bar and skated into the deserted centre of the rink. He whirled around aimlessly for a couple of minutes.

"When does he start to skate?" the man demanded.

"I'll make him if you want," the Manager said. He leaned over and pushed a button on the disco unit, changing the record. Suddenly Benjamin came alive, shooting around the ice at high speed. Then he did a couple of flashy jumps, showing off.

"Is he the one you're looking for?" the Manager asked.

"He could be." The man shrugged. "I'm going down on the ice."

Benjamin tried a few of his more difficult moves, then went over to study two other skaters who were using the middle of the ice. Since Benjamin was eight all his moves had been copied off other skaters.

He almost ran the man down. He was standing in the centre of the rink staring at Benjamin and for some reason he wasn't wearing skates. Benjamin whizzed round him, did a spiral and a very bad double jump, then went off into a spin. When he came out of it, he checked the marks left on the ice to see if he'd moved across the ice on the spin, a very bad fault. He grinned. It was the best he'd done for weeks. He turned casually to see if the man was still watching and when he saw that he was, he tried one of his favourite moves, an inside Spread Eagle, a simple glide with the toes pointed outwards. He tried to extend it so that he went right round the man and when he just failed, he covered up by leaning forward and picking up speed. Still the man watched him.

Benjamin casually circled the ice, then shot across the centre and tried a triple jump right in front of the man. The landing wasn't too bad. Benjamin felt pleased—a triple jump is one of the moves that sorts out the good skaters from the bad. Benjamin tried another double while trying to keep the man in view and was rewarded by missing the landing completely. He just caught himself and skated off, feeling embarrassed.

After another half hour of the man's gaze, Benjamin had had enough of trying to impress him. He skated to the edge of the ice and stamped away to return his skates. Benjamin made sure the girl hid them beneath the counter for him, then, deciding that for once he simply must afford something to eat, he went upstairs to the cafeteria.

The shepherd's pie was on special offer so after studying the contents of his pockets he ordered that and a Coke to go with it. He carried his plate to the table overlooking the rink and started to eat.

Someone put a cup of coffee opposite him and sat down. Benjamin grunted. He didn't like eating with strangers.

"Tell me then son, who are you trying to be?" a voice demanded. "Eric Heiden or Robin Cousins?"

Benjamin looked up in surprise. It was the man without the skates.

"I beg your pardon?" he said carefully.

"I was asking about your skating ambitions."

"I haven't any skating ambitions."

The man snorted. "You just come here to mess about, do you?"

"That's right."

"Two nights a week, every week?"

"I like messing about." Benjamin wished the man would go away.

"I'm a trainer," the man said suddenly.

Benjamin shrugged. "Everybody has to make a living, don't they?"

"I asked you what your skating ambitions were." the man persisted.

"You're the trainer—you tell me."

"Okay then, I will." The man leaned back in his chair. "You'll never be a speed skater if that's what you want. You haven't the build. You're too tall and slim."

Benjamin smiled at him, not at all put out.

"More the build of a figure skater," the man went on. "In fact, if you tried very hard, you would make a reasonable figure skater but not, I fear, ever in the top echelon. It's too late, you see. You should have spent the last five years doing compulsory figures. I bet you've never skated a figure in your life, have you?"

"And I'm not about to start now," Benjamin said. "I enjoy skating, so just leave me to it, will you?" He gestured to the plate in front of him. "This shepherd's pie's not up to much but it's taken all my cash, so let me concentrate on it."

The man sipped his coffee and carried on as if Benjamin hadn't said a word.

"There is a branch of the sport you could take to the top, and I do mean the top."

"Don't tell me—ice-cream man."

The man ignored this. "Who taught you to skate?" he demanded.

"My mother," Benjamin said. "She was killed in a car crash when I was eight."

"Oh, yes."

"How do you mean, yes?"

"I mean every move you do out there," the man gestured towards the rink, "you skate as though there was a partner at your side."

"Rubbish."

"I assure you it's not noticeable to most people."

"But it is to you?"

"Oh yes." The man leaned forward. "The thing is, you do it rather well—when you're not showing off, that is."

Benjamin grinned.

"I've a young girl under training who needs a partner," the man said reasonably. "I think you might do, otherwise I wouldn't be wasting my time talking to you."

"You think I might do?"

"Yes."

"That's big of you."

The man reached into his jacket pocket and produced a measuring tape.

"Hold out your arm," he said.

"What for?" Benjamin demanded.

"I want to measure your arm."

"Why?"

"Look, just let me measure your arm. Humour me."

"You need it, pal," Benjamin muttered. Resignedly he held out his arm, and the man ran the tape along it. For the first time he looked pleased. He put the tape away and sat down again.

"Good," he said. "You see, if your arms are much longer than hers then it leaves an ugly line when you skate together."

"Just let's hang on a minute, now I've passed the physical—what branch of skating are we talking about?"

"Ice dancing."

"Oh come on," Benjamin said, disgusted. He stood up and the man rose with him.

"One last thing," the man said. Benjamin paused and the man went on, "Jayne Torvill and Christopher Dean are on television tonight at eleven o'clock."

"So?"

"So go home and watch them. You like watching skating, don't you? Then, if you're interested, come and see me here, the day after tomorrow."

"I won't be."

"We'll see—ask at the door for Morris."

"Wednesday's closed night."

"Not to everybody. You just mention my name." Benjamin shrugged and turned away.

"Oh and Benjamin, Wednesday night or never— you only get the one chance." The man gave him a nod then limped away.

Benjamin stood frozen, wondering how the man knew his name.

3

A Surprise Meeting

It was four o'clock and the school was emptying with an efficiency that the pupils only demonstrated out of school hours. Benjamin wandered into the changing rooms to find Rob frantically rummaging through the locker they shared.

"My boots, I can't find my boots," Rob said angrily.

"Your rugby boots?" Benjamin asked.

"Of course, somebody's nicked them—yours are here." Rob held up a pair of rugby boots thick with mud.

"It's only a practice game, isn't it?"

"That's hardly the point, is it. Do you expect me to play in bare feet?"

"The way you're playing lately you'd win all the same."

"Eh?" Rob turned to him, a blank look on his face.

"Yes, I have nothing but admiration for your game recently, your speed, your tactics, your passes—awe-inspiring."

"Oh yes—what do you want?" Rob demanded.

"Want?" Benjamin said in a hurt voice. "Aren't I allowed to congratulate somebody who must surely be the best rugby player in the school?"

"I said what do you want?"

"A quid."

"Oh is that all?" Rob reached into his pocket and handed Benjamin a pound coin.

"Thanks, you can have it back Friday."

"What's it for?" asked Rob who was turning the contents of the locker out on to the floor. "Got a date?"

"I have in a way, at the rink—tonight."

"The hell you have, you're playing rugby."

"Gaskins says he'll stand in for me."

"You can stuff Gaskins, you're playing and that's the end of it."

"Can't be done I'm afraid, I really do have to go to the rink."

"You must be off your head. You're willing to miss a practice game to go pratting around on the ice?"

"As you said, it's a practice game, it doesn't matter," Benjamin said.

"There's a game Saturday. Does that matter?" Rob said hotly.

"I'll be there Saturday."

"I only hope I can find you a place in the team." Rob went back to the locker. Benjamin stood looking at him for a moment, then he said,

"I suppose this means I'm definitely off your Christmas card list?"

"Rats—I hope you break a leg."

"Oh well, do your best without me," Benjamin said from the door. Rob turned and hurled a boot at him. Benjamin ducked and watched it go past.

"There you are, you found them," he said. "That was one of yours."

Benjamin didn't need his entrance fee. The name Morris magically opened the door for him. He stood feeling self-conscious as the girl behind the desk picked up a microphone and paged Morris.

Some minutes later Morris came limping up the stairs to the reception. He signalled to the girl. "It's all right—he's with me."

"You decided to come then?" he said to Benjamin.

"Looks like it."

"You watched the programme like I said?"

"Yeh—it wasn't bad." Morris stood gazing at him in silence—waiting. "Okay," Benjamin said. "It was brilliant."

Morris nodded. "Good," he said. "Now, where are your skates?"

"I hire them."

"You don't have your own skates?"

"No, I don't." Benjamin was more angry than embarrassed. "Have you any idea what those things cost? They're over fifty pounds a pair."

"You can double that for a good pair," Morris said.

"Well I don't have that kind of money. Anyway the girl at the booth keeps a special pair for me."

"All right," Morris said, "go and help yourself from the booth. There won't be anyone there tonight. I'll be on the practice rink—you know where that is?"

Benjamin nodded.

"Don't waste time. Your partner's waiting to meet you."

Some five minutes later Benjamin was standing outside a door marked "PRIVATE" at the end of the main rink. He took a deep breath, opened it and marched in. There was a pause, then:

"Oh no, not him. He can't even stay on his feet in ordinary shoes." Belinda Thomas, head in the air, hand on one hip, stood in the middle of the training rink glaring at him.

For once Benjamin was lost for words.

"Wait till you've seen him skate," Morris snapped. Belinda shrugged.

Morris nodded to Benjamin, who stepped warily on to the ice.

"You obviously know each other," Morris said.

"We're in the same form," Belinda said. "He's the resident idiot."

"And she's the resident smart ass," Benjamin said, suddenly finding his voice. They glared at each other.

"Right, now we've established a friendly relationship," Morris interrupted them, "let's get down to business. Benjamin, Belinda's not going to take you seriously until she's seen you skate."

"I didn't realize I was on trial," Benjamin muttered.

He glided forward, then, finding the rink bigger than it looked, he flew round it a couple of times and finished with a shower of ice in a dead stop.

"Great," said Belinda. She turned to Morris. "We going in for Barrel Jumping now, Morris?"

"No, we're going to jump over your mouth," Benjamin said, annoyed. "That'll be a lot more difficult."

Morris gestured to the small patch of ice. "I reckon there's enough room to do a triple there," he said to Benjamin. "What do you think?"

Without another word he flashed round the rink then took off, spinning round three times before he landed on one skate.

Morris looked at Belinda. "That was a triple," he said.

"That was a very bad triple," she snapped.

"Can you do one?" he demanded. She gazed at him for a long moment then looked away without answering. Morris beckoned to Benjamin.

"How much dancing have you done?" Morris asked him.

"None—and I'm not ashamed of it."

"You were doing some dance steps the other night, I saw you."

Benjamin shrugged. "If I was I didn't realize they were ice dancing steps."

"It doesn't matter, let's get started," Morris said.

"Will you tell Zebedee here that we don't go springing all over the shop in ice dancing?" Belinda said sarcastically.

"Just get on the ice, will you," Morris snapped, "and if you've got chewing gum in your mouth, swallow it, now."

"I haven't," she said.

Morris showed Benjamin how to hold his new

partner. He stood embarrassed as Morris positioned his hands more accurately.

"Now we've got to get you used to each other," Morris said, "so for the first few nights you're going to skate some nice easy steps and you're not going to try and outdo each other."

They glided around the ice very cautiously at first. Benjamin was surprised at how easily Belinda followed him, keeping her skates well out of the way. As Morris had suspected, she was chewing some gum. Benjamin couldn't help but admire the way she automatically stopped chewing every time she was facing Morris.

"Doesn't he like chewing gum?" Benjamin asked quietly.

"No, he says you can choke on it if you fall over," Belinda said, the first polite remark she had made that night.

"I suppose you could," Benjamin said.

"You might—I don't fall over," she said.

After that they skated round in silence except for Morris's instructions. Benjamin was using steps he had been doing for years but they had become so much more difficult now he had a partner to consider. He kept wanting to break away to do a few jumps or some fast skating but Belinda was holding on to him, keeping him to the same boring routine.

"Can't we try something more difficult?" he asked her after nearly an hour.

She gazed at him unsmiling. "I think that's a bad idea," she said.

"Why?"

"Because Morris hasn't told us to."

"Is he always like that?" Benjamin demanded, trying to keep the conversation going.

"How do you mean?"

"So miserable—he never smiles."

"He's in a good mood tonight."

"Hell." Benjamin stopped by Morris. "She says we mustn't do anything more difficult," he said.

"Not just yet," Morris said.

"Why not? I've been doing this for years, one two, one two, then a simple three turn. I'm not a beginner you know."

"You are to ice dancing. You've got to learn to skate with a partner. At the moment your rhythm's wrong, you're half a beat ahead of Belinda, and those simple three turns you sneer at are a mess."

"Oh—right." Benjamin gave a shrug and started leading the way around the ice again. After a minute their eyes met.

"It's probably you going too slow," he said. She didn't answer, just gave him her most sardonic look.

After another hour Benjamin had had enough. It was much harder work than it looked and he was getting more and more frustrated with himself, his skates simply would not do what he wanted them to do.

At long last Morris called a halt.

"That'll do for tonight," he said. "Now, if we're going to do this I need you three nights a week, and one of them must be Wednesday."

"Well I usually skate Monday and Friday," Benjamin said.

"Is that all right for you?" Morris asked Belinda. She was studying her nails.

"Anything you say," she said offhandedly.

"I'll see you Friday then," Morris said. They went to the changing rooms. Benjamin deliberately took his time. He wanted to give Belinda a chance to get off home. He felt awkward about meeting her away from Morris, but when he got outside she was waiting for him.

"Don't rush yourself," she said. "The bus is at ten o'clock, you know."

"I came by bike."

"By bike!" she said aghast. "But it's so far."

"Oh it's not too bad, I'm quite used to it."

"But the bus is much quicker. You don't live far from me, do you?" Belinda protested.

"Not far—no."

"Well, you can't be giving your best if you have a hard ride beforehand."

"It's really very simple," Benjamin said. "I haven't got the bus fare. It's all I can do to pay the entrance money."

Belinda was silent.

"My dad doesn't like me skating," Benjamin went on. "He thinks it's soft."

"What's he going to say about you switching to ice dancing?" Belinda asked.

"I dread to think. He won't give me any money for skating now and Morris says I need my own skates."

"One pair at least."

"Well there's no hope of that," Benjamin said. "It's not that he's mean—if it was rugby boots I could have them tomorrow."

An embarrassed silence hung between them. They had hardly spoken all night without insulting each other and now there was no one else with them, strangely they felt they had to be more polite.

Benjamin made an effort. "I didn't know you skated," he said. "I've never seen you here before."

"We were skating over at Wolverhampton until last week," she said. "Then Morris heard they had a practice rink here so we moved over." Then in a slightly more friendly voice she added, "I knew you skated."

"It's no secret," Benjamin said, sensing a snub. None came.

They reached the railings to which Benjamin's bike was chained.

"Hang on a sec," he said, "I'll walk you to the stop."

She shook her head. "I know the way, thank you."

"If you say so."

"I'll see you Friday night then."

"Tomorrow morning you mean."

"Tomorrow morning—oh yes."

Benjamin unlocked the padlock and swung his leg over the crossbar.

"Benjamin." He looked up. It was the first time she had ever used his proper name.

"Yes?"

"You're not a bad skater."

Benjamin gazed after her as she faded into the darkness.

Meanwhile Morris was walking around the ice. At one end of the rink, just where Benjamin and Belinda had been turning, there were deep marks left in the surface of the ice. He knelt carefully and studied them for a long time. Finally he got to his feet, lost in thought. Suddenly he smiled.

4

Wheels within Wheels

Belinda totally ignored Benjamin all the next day. Benjamin, who had never yet found the courage to ask any of the girls out, had been looking forward to showing off his friendship with the most attractive girl in the fourth year.

"Who the hell does she think she is?" he muttered.

"Eh—who are you on about?" Rob asked, surprised. They were in the bike sheds and Rob was strapping a briefcase full of homework to his bike.

"Belinda Thomas."

"Oh—why?"

"No reason," Benjamin said. "I've just realized that I dislike her intensely."

"You asked her out," Rob said excitedly.

"No, I did not," Benjamin said, "and I'm not about to—not ever."

"You're probably right," Rob said. "I'm not sure you're quite ready for Belinda Thomas just yet."

"Rats."

"No, I'm quite serious. Now there's a nice little girl in Four East should suit you—kind, homely sort of girl."

"Go and fall off your bike," Benjamin snapped. He rode off leaving Rob behind, laughing.

Belinda seemed more friendly on Friday night. Morris was just as demanding. Straight away, he started them on the same steps as the previous session. For the first half an hour they were enthusiastic enough but then boredom set in and Morris could see their skating start to suffer. He called them to the side.

"That'll do for the Waltz for now," he said.

"Is that we were doing—the Waltz?" Benjamin asked.

"Trying to do," Morris said. "It'll be months before you start getting it right."

"Well, how many dances are there?"

"There are four different Waltzes for a start, and that's just the compulsories," Morris said.

"Then there's Polka, Blues, Rumba, Quickstep, Tango—do you want me to go on?" Belinda said callously.

"This is going to take years," Benjamin said bleakly.

"She's leading you on—you don't have to do them all, you have to choose three from four groups."

"It's a bit complicated, isn't it?" Benjamin said.

"You just wait till you see the marking if you think that's complicated," Belinda said.

"Don't worry about it," Morris said. "Now we'll go on to the Quickstep for a bit."

Belinda pulled a face. "Ugh, Quickstep," she said.

"It can't be worse than the Waltz," Benjamin said.

"Oh yes it can—I can't get the rotations right."

"What rotations?" Benjamin asked.

"The Twizzles," Morris said. He waved Belinda on to the ice. She sighed, skated a few steps, then did a simple rotation on the back foot with her front knee raised. It looked clumsy. Benjamin stepped on to the ice and tried the same move.

"Like that?" he said, executing the move perfectly. "And that's ice dancing is it?" Morris turned away to hide a smile. Belinda looked extremely put out.

"Perhaps we should change positions," she snapped. "Can you skate backwards as well—Einstein?"

Benjamin, who had just been trying the move out, didn't realize what she was getting at. Hurriedly Morris started them off around the ice again, trying out the Quickstep. Benjamin enjoyed this much more, the faster tempo more in keeping with his skating. Belinda didn't get on so well. She kept fluffing the rotations. Try as she might, they simply wouldn't come right. As the evening wore on, she got crosser and crosser and finally she tried too hard and spun over, nearly taking Benjamin with her.

There was a silence, then Benjamin said, "Good job you're not chewing gum, isn't it?"

Belinda scrambled to her feet and stormed over to him, looking dangerous.

"All right calm down," Morris said. He glanced at his watch. "It's half past nine. Let's call it a night, shall we?"

He took them upstairs for a cup of coffee.

Belinda sat by Morris, Benjamin opposite them.

"Well?" Morris said, aiming it at Benjamin.

Benjamin jumped. "Well what?" he asked, surprised.

"Well, are you going to stay the course?" Belinda answered for Morris.

"I guess so," Benjamin said, carefully.

"As long as you realize the work it's going to entail," Morris said.

"I enjoy skating, and it's only one extra night, isn't it?"

"For the moment maybe, but I want you both to start fitness training as well," said Morris. "I had to give up figure skating because of the arthritis in my knees. That was twenty years ago but I'm still fitter than either of you two. You're going to have to start a regime of exercises."

Benjamin and Belinda looked at each other and grimaced, feeling an amity for the first time. Morris ignored their glance.

"I'll supply you both with a schedule to work to," he said.

"Benjamin already does a lot of cycling," Belinda said callously.

"Good, then that means that only you will have to get a bike, doesn't it?" Morris cut her down.

"I can't ride a bike!"

"You'll soon learn." Morris could be equally callous. "It's one of the best forms of exercise and it'll help you lose a few pounds—you could do with it."

Benjamin grinned at Belinda's furious face. There

was an icy silence as they drank their coffee, then Morris turned to Benjamin.

"How old were you when you first went on the ice?" he asked.

"I'm not sure," Benjamin said. "My mother taught me to skate. She was a figure skater."

"I know," Morris said.

"How?" Benjamin asked, surprised.

"I was her trainer."

Benjamin was dumbstruck, Belinda unconcerned. She had obviously known.

"I knew who you were the first night I saw you skate," Morris said, "especially when you did that inside Spread Eagle."

"Why?"

"Well, they've gone out of fashion. I haven't seen one in five years, they all do outside Spreads nowadays."

"So what?"

"It was your mother's favourite move. No one ever did it better." Morris stood up. "I've got to go," he said, then he looked hard at Benjamin. "Your mother was a marvellous skater," he said.

"I know," said Benjamin. Then he added, "If she'd lived she could have been a world champion."

"She might well have been," Morris said. "She was one of the best skaters I've ever seen." He nodded to each of them, then marched away.

Benjamin looked at Belinda. "He knew my mother," he said.

"Yes."

"You knew?"

"It was one of the reasons we moved from Wolverhampton."

"You went to a lot of trouble."

"Mm, he's been looking for a partner for me for over a year now—he says the most important thing with ice dancing is to have the right partner."

"And he thinks I'll do in spite of never having done any ice dancing before?"

Belinda stood up. "Look, I must go," she said. "We haven't all got our own transport."

"Belinda."

"Yes." She paused.

"I'll do my very best, that's all I can say."

She gave a sigh. "Don't be so daft," she said crossly. "It's not a question of you keeping up with me—it's me keeping up with you."

And so it went on. Three nights a week, the constant practice and slowly, oh so slowly, the new steps were introduced until they were truly dancing together. Three nights a week Belinda treated Benjamin with friendly reserve and five days a week she acted as if he didn't exist.

Every morning both followed a strict regime of exercises followed by a six-kilometre run. Every evening Benjamin wasn't skating he went out on his bike, looking for hills to ride up. They became fitter and fitter and soon they were skating a fairly long programme without undue strain.

Their social life began to suffer and Benjamin began to find it more and more difficult to keep up with his homework. Four North and Four South were expected to do about two hours homework a night and now for three nights Benjamin could do none at all and on the other nights he had to fit in some training. Caustic comments were being made by his teachers but Benjamin refused to give any reasons. Belinda never mentioned to anyone what they were doing and Benjamin decided that if she was ashamed of him then he wasn't about to say anything.

One Friday morning, Mrs Hopkins took them by surprise.

Mrs Hopkins had been their form mistress since they had first come together as a form in the second year. Each year was split into five forms, North, South, East, West and Centre. The South forms tended to be where the misfits were put: the children who seemed clever but never did any work, the ones who were brilliant in one subject but useless at everything else, anyone particularly good at sport and, inevitably, the troublemakers.

As a new teacher Mrs Hopkins had ended up with a South form, who were obviously a "difficult" form. After a few months she had turned her form into one that was respected throughout the school, aided by the natural leaders that had emerged; Benjamin, Rob Stevens, Chris Jenkins, Barbara Wallace and Josey Law.

Form teachers tend to change each year but when, at the beginning of the fourth year, the Headmaster had tried to replace Mrs Hopkins, much against her wishes, Benjamin and Rob Stevens had led Four South out "on strike" and they had sat in the quad until the Headmaster had wisely changed his mind.

Mrs Hopkins always encouraged a discussion with

her form each morning before Assembly. It was one of the ways in which she had built up a friendly atmosphere.

Benjamin was secretly doing some homework when the words "ice dancing" caught his attention. He listened with amazement as Mrs Hopkins told them about the skating she had seen on television the night before.

"It just has to be the best form of skating," Mrs Hopkins was saying. "Now I know some of you do go skating, but has anybody ever done any ice dancing?"

Benjamin, who never put up his hand in class, wasn't going to begin now. He glanced over at Belinda. She was studying her hands as usual. Benjamin hid behind Chris and frowned.

"Blow her," he muttered. "I suppose she doesn't want her precious friends to know about me." He went back to his homework.

Belinda was actually watching Benjamin from beneath her eyelashes. She gave a sigh when he went back to his writing without attempting to join the discussion. "Oh well," she thought, "I suppose ice dancing isn't macho enough for his friends to know about."

The bell for Assembly put an end to any more discussion and the class started to break up. Benjamin had stopped going to Assembly in the third form. He usually hid in the storeroom and read or played cards, if he could persuade one of the others to join him. Nowadays though, he had to use the time to catch up on some homework. He was sitting in the tiny room copying Rob's Maths when a tap on the door nearly made him jump out of his skin. The door opened and Belinda walked in.

"What on earth do you want?" he stammered.

"Just a word if I may, Benjamin."

"You're missing Assembly," he said.

She grinned. "Oh I usually cut Assembly—I go to the cloakrooms, with some of the others."

"You do?" Benjamin said shocked. "I thought I was the only one who did that."

"Morris phoned last night."

"What about—has he had enough of us?" Benjamin was only half joking.

"Hardly, he's a bit worried about you cycling over each night. I mean he wants you to be fit, but a hard ride just before a session affects your skating."

"I know it does. Some nights I'm tired before I go on the ice, but what do you want me to do? You know how my dad feels about skating. He's not about to give me any bus fare and he sure as hell isn't going to run me over to Halesowen three times a week."

"Yes, we know that. Why do you think Morris rang me and not you? He didn't want to stir up any more trouble for you at home. Look, the manager of the rink has agreed to let us off our entrance money."

"Has he—why?"

"Morris talked him round, I suppose. Anyway Morris said that the money you save should just about cover the bus fare over."

"I suppose it would," Benjamin said slowly.

"Well, what do you think?"

"Yes, well—great. I'll come by bus then."

"Good. I'll meet you by the bus stop at six tonight."

"I'll come round for you if you like."

"Benjamin, I'll meet you by the stop."

"Okay."

She nodded at him and went to the door. She paused.

"Benjamin," she said.

"Yeh?"

"My dad would give us both a lift. He used to take me over but he can't do it now."

"That's okay."

"He's lost his licence."

"Oh." Benjamin didn't know what to say.

"Nobody else in the school knows that," she said coldly. She pointed a finger at him. "You'd better make sure it stays that way."

She closed the door on Benjamin with a bang.

5

Potential Champions

Benjamin had been wondering what they would talk about on the bus, but immediately Belinda sat down she produced some homework and proceeded to study all the way to the rink.

Morris was waiting for them on the practice rink. Right away he unleashed a bombshell.

"You need your own skates," he said to Benjamin.

"Oh no, not again," Benjamin said worriedly. "I just can't afford them, Morris."

"You have to afford them," Morris said. "You can't improve till you have a pair fitted for you."

"I really haven't the money," Benjamin said earnestly, "and what with all the training I can't even get a part-time job." He paused, then, "I used to work at a garage three nights a week but I gave it up when we started."

"You gave up your job to skate?" Belinda said, startled.

"Yes, of course."

Morris looked pleased. "We'll have to find the money somehow," he said.

"I suppose I could sell something," said Benjamin, "and I might be able to pick up a second-hand pair cheap—they sometimes have them on sale here."

"That's no good, ice dancing skates aren't the same as normal skates," Morris said.

"Aren't they?" Benjamin said, surprised.

"Where have you been all your life?" Belinda said with a sigh. "The blade on a dancing skate is much narrower."

"Point three of an inch," Morris added.

"Look," Belinda lifted up her foot and showed him the blade of her skate.

"Oh yes, much narrower," said Benjamin, out of his depth. "That's probably why you keep falling over."

"Don't push your luck," Belinda said. Benjamin turned back to Morris.

"So it's a question of raising a hundred quid?" he asked.

"Less than that. I can get them wholesale."

Benjamin thought for a moment, then shook his head. "I really don't see how I can do it," he said. "I could try to sell my bike but it's not worth much."

"You need it for training anyway," Belinda said.

"Well," Morris said, "it's not just your problem, is it? It's our problem as well, we're a team—the three of us."

"Of course," Belinda said. "Surely we can raise the cash between us?"

"No way," Benjamin said. "I'm not taking your money."

"Sentiments like that are for people who can afford them," Morris said crossly. "Now do as you're told. We aren't about to let your daft pride waste all our efforts."

"Yes but . . ." Benjamin tried to protest.

"But nothing!" Belinda snapped. "If you can't let your friends help then you can go to blazes."

"All right, all right." Benjamin held up his hands defensively.

"A third each," Morris said. Belinda nodded and after a second so did Benjamin.

Benjamin followed the others on to the ice, lost in his thoughts. The skates didn't matter that much, nor did the money—Belinda had called him a friend.

For some time now they had been putting together the rudiments of a free programme. Morris brought along a huge cassette recorder and they tried fitting some of their strong points to the music. By now they had mastered many of the basic steps, Belinda finding it hard to believe she once found the rotations difficult.

After one record they stopped in front of Morris, panting for breath.

"That was great," Benjamin gasped, "that fits our fast section just right."

"It did go quite well," said Morris, stopping the cassette.

"What was it?" Benjamin asked.

"I'll have a look," said Morris.

"It was 'Wanted'," Belinda said.

"Eh?" Benjamin said.

"It's the instrumental version of 'Wanted'—by the Dooleys."

"How do you know?" Benjamin asked.

"I happen to like the Dooleys."

"You do? I thought they were dead."

"You didn't find it so bad to dance to, did you?" she demanded.

"No—it's a good record, let's keep it in."

Morris nodded. He ran the cassette back and they went through the routine again. Every time their eyes met Belinda stuck her tongue out at him. They skated to a halt, there was a silence, then Benjamin looked at Morris.

"They're a good group, the Dooleys," he said.

The following morning, Benjamin was frantically trying to do his Maths homework in time for the first lesson with Mr Coup. He was sitting in the store-room scribbling away when there was a tap on the door. This time he didn't jump.

Belinda walked in.

"I need somewhere to do some work," she said, defensively.

"Oh," Benjamin said, surprised. "I thought you went to the cloakrooms in Assembly."

"They're too crowded." She smiled. "More people seem to cut Assembly than actually go nowadays."

"Well, sit down," Benjamin said, coming to his feet. "You'd better have this chair, it's from out of the staff room."

"I'll bet it is," she said. "You have it. You went to the trouble of pinching it."

Belinda dragged in an ordinary chair and they worked side by side on the low shelf that ran across the tiny room.

"Coffee?" said Benjamin, after a minute's silence.

"Eh?" Belinda said, then she started to laugh. "You haven't got a kettle in here?"

"Certainly. All mod cons." He boiled the kettle and poured them both coffee in real cups.

"Milk? Sugar?" he asked, airily.

"Just milk please," she said. "Where do you get the stuff from?"

"Oh I take a stroll through the kitchens once a week," he said. "Now you should have come on Monday. They'd just had some Garibaldis in."

"I'm on a diet, remember?"

"Oh yes, Morris does rather seem to rule our lives just lately."

She smiled, "He's all right, Morris."

"Yes, and he's almost half human as well," Benjamin said.

"He's just a little dedicated that's all."

"Of course," Benjamin said at once. "I happen to think quite a lot of him."

"I'm glad," she said, pleased. "I've known him for some years—he's always been the same."

"He's been training you for that long?" Benjamin asked, surprised.

"Oh sure. My dad used to pay for lessons twice a week."

"Does he still pay him?"

"No," she said, then added a little reluctantly, "he stopped charging when you came along."

"Oh." There was an embarrassed silence, broken by the bell.

"There—I've not done a stroke," she sighed, "and

Baggy Stokes will go up the wall if I'm late with my homework again."

"Never mind, I've hardly done any for her all term," Benjamin said. He gathered up his books and quickly hid away the kettle and coffee cups.

"Would you mind if I come again tomorrow?" she asked, studying her nails intently. "I've got so much homework built up, I really must get some done."

"Of course you can." Benjamin gave a grin. "I'm almost glad to hear it. I couldn't work out how you were managing to get it all done. If Coup asks for the homework at the start of the lesson I'm done for."

The morning break found Benjamin scribbling lines furiously. Rob was sitting beside him doing the second hundred. They finished almost at the same moment.

"You're going to have to stop upsetting Coup," Rob said wearily. "I'm getting cheesed off helping with your lines—I mean it's every week just lately."

"Well you see it takes less time to do the lines than it does to do the homework," Benjamin said reasonably.

"I thought he was going to make it detention this time."

"No—he quite likes me really."

"Oh yes he sounded like he did," Rob said sarcastically. "Anyhow, you couldn't get stuck in detention this week; there's a match on Thursday."

Benjamin sighed. "I'm not sure I can."

"Oh yes you can," Rob said quickly. "It's against Tregorath and I'm afraid Gaskins just won't do."

"If I must," Benjamin said. He looked up as three girls brushed past. One of them was Belinda. Josey

Law and Amanda Smith smiled at Rob, Belinda gave Benjamin her half grin—it was the first time she had smiled at him in school.

"When you've quite finished with that girl you dislike so much," Rob said, "we were discussing rugby."

"No—you were."

"Yes, well, the match is for the Shield, so you can just forget anything else you happen to have on that night."

"I've said I will."

"I just don't get you, Benjamin, you haven't been to a practice for weeks. If it was anyone else I'd drop them like a shot."

"I've scored points the last three Saturdays. What more do you want?" Benjamin demanded.

"You're not the same." Rob shook his head. "Six months ago when you had that twisted ankle you threw a fit when I tried to replace you. You turned up for the game so strapped up you looked like a survivor from a plane crash—what's come over you lately?"

"Oh stuff," Benjamin said shortly. "Come on, I really can't be late for Chemistry again."

Benjamin sat in a pool of mud, nursing his eye. It was Thursday evening and they were on the rugby field playing Tregorath. The game was nearly over and they were leading by sixteen points to nine. Benjamin had scored once and Rob had converted it for him, but after that the captain of the opposing team, a huge boy, had marked Benjamin and tackled him at every opportunity, whether he had the ball or not.

Benjamin had just tried his sidestep, but the captain of Tregorath had stopped him by the simple method of punching him in the eye, out of sight of the referee.

The whistle went for a scrum down and Rob came running up.

"You all right?" he demanded.

"No—I want a blood transfusion."

"You can have one later. Now get up and play, will you?" Benjamin climbed to his feet and sprinted to his position next to Rob.

"You know the Incredible Hulk there," Benjamin pointed.

"The captain. What about him?" Rob asked.

"He's mine," Benjamin said. "Next time he gets the ball leave him to me." Rob gave an evil laugh, then the ball came free and they were off again. Benjamin got to it first but was brought down before he could get going.

"C'mon Trueman, what are you playing at?" came Mr Lander's roar, but Benjamin had spotted something that spurred him on much more than the sports master's voice. Belinda Thomas was standing with Josey Law watching the game.

The captain of Tregorath was lumbering up the field clasping the ball when the heel of Benjamin's palm came up under his chin so hard it left him sitting in the mud counting stars. Benjamin was away, running like a sprinter. He cut across the field, leaving the rest of the pack still going the wrong way. Rob ran with him but soon fell back. Benjamin jinked around two opposing players, leaving them for fools, then he was over the touch line.

"Put that ball down!" came Lander's roar. Benjamin pretended he hadn't heard. Stopping suddenly, he let one of the opposing backs overrun him, then he strolled casually on and placed the ball in the exact centre of the posts.

He trotted off, avoiding Mr Lander's infuriated gaze. Lander hated people playing to the gallery. Seconds later, just as Rob converted, the final whistle blew.

"Now that was the old Benjamin Trueman," Rob said as they trooped wearily back to the dressing room, "though I should stay out of Dicky Lander's way for a while if I were you."

"No sweat. I saw him do that at a county match once," Benjamin grinned, "and he knows it."

"Did you see who was watching?" Rob asked.

"No—who?"

"Belinda Thomas and Josey Law, that's who. I've never seen them at a match before."

"Oh," Benjamin said.

"Wonder why they turned up tonight," Rob mused.

"Probably nothing better to do," said Benjamin.

Rob gave Benjamin a hard look then walked away laughing to himself.

"Oh, now that is nice," Morris said as Benjamin walked on to the practice rink the following evening.

Benjamin rubbed his black eye self-consciously.

"I think it's an improvement," said Belinda.

"Yes, I can see it now," Morris said, "the packed stands, the soft music, suddenly the announcer's voice breaks through the hubbub," his voice rose, "and the next contestants are Belinda Thomas and Benjamin Trueman—and up you glide, dressed immaculately—with a dirty great black eye."

Benjamin grinned. "It's a good job we're only practising."

"Isn't it?" said Morris. "It so happens we are going to go on to the big rink once a week, so if you could refrain from falling out with people, it would add somewhat to your performance."

"I didn't get it fighting, Morris," protested Benjamin. "I got it playing rugby."

"Rugby?" Morris demanded. His bantering tone disappeared.

"Yes, rugby," Benjamin said, puzzled.

"You idiot," Morris said angrily.

"Eh?"

"You think I'm wasting my time training you each week, to see you laid off for a month with a broken arm?"

"I'm sorry, Morris, I didn't think," Benjamin said soberly.

"And you." Morris turned to Belinda. "Didn't you think either?"

"Of course," she said reluctantly, "but off the ice Benjamin's a law to himself."

Morris turned back to Benjamin. "Give it up," he said.

"Pardon?"

"Give—it—up!" Morris said, very distinctly. "Never—ever, while I am your trainer, will you play rugby again."

"Well, okay Morris," Benjamin said, "but Rob's not going to like it."

43

"Rob, whoever the hell he is, doesn't travel thirty kilometres, three nights a week to give his valuable training free."

"We both appreciate it very much," Belinda said quietly.

"I do not wish to be appreciated."

There was a silence. Benjamin broke it.

"Morris, you usually get paid for training, don't you?"

"How else do you think I make a living?" Morris demanded. "I spend every morning of the week from six till nine training people, I give private lessons most afternoons, they come to me from all over the world—but the evenings I leave free for you, and you risk it all by playing rugby."

"I don't understand then, Morris," Benjamin said. "Why do you bother with us, I mean what do you get out of it?"

"Get out of it?" Morris said. He paused for a minute, then very slowly and quietly, he said, "What I get out of it is the pleasure and possibly the kudos of training a couple of potential champions."

"Are we that good?" Belinda asked softly.

"You could be," Morris said, "given time and a very great deal of work."

Benjamin held out his hands to Belinda.

"C'mon," he said, "let's get going."

6

Benjamin does his Equations

It took till the second lesson after morning break on
Monday for Benjamin to pluck up the courage to tell
Rob he could no longer play rugby.

"You're having me on," Rob said in disbelief.

"I'm not—look, we've won all the major games for
the Shield, you won't miss me."

"I don't get this. This is rugby we're talking
about."

"I just haven't the time, Rob. You know how far
behind I am with my work."

"That never worried you before."

"Well it does now, our GCSEs are next year, you
know."

"And you can't even spare the odd Saturday
morning?"

"No—I've told you why."

"You haven't, not the real reason anyway. I bet
you still find time to go skating, don't you?"

"Not as much as I'd like."

"Rubbish! I don't know what's happened to you lately—you know it was the form debate last night?"

"Was it? How did we get on?" Benjamin asked.

"Do you care? You didn't bother to show your face, did you?"

"Of course I care."

"We lost by two votes, yours and Belinda Thomas's. I don't know where she was but I expect she had a good excuse—you know how these things go, it doesn't matter how well the debaters speak. Four East won because their whole form turned up to vote."

"Oh," Benjamin said quietly.

"Last year you punched Reegie's head because he forgot to come—you going to let him punch yours now?"

"I didn't forget. I had to go out."

"You went skating. You always go skating on a Friday."

"Well, what if I did?" Benjamin said, aggrieved.

"Remember in the third you calling that meeting and telling us all to stick together, you know when they were trying to put some of us in Three Centre—or when you led us out on strike when the head tried to replace Mrs Hopkins?"

"Of course I do—what's that got to do with it?"

"Or the time when Reegie let off that firework in Mr Coup's lesson? The whole form was in detention for weeks yet no one told on him."

"What are you getting at?"

"What I'm getting at is this—I only hope Reegie doesn't do it again—I'm not sure we could rely on you if your skating was in danger."

"You want to mind what you're saying," Benjamin said hotly, "before I forget you're a friend."

"Falling out with me won't make any difference," Rob said, shaking his head. "I just don't think you're one of us any more."

They sat in silence awaiting the arrival of Mrs Hopkins and the start of French. Resignedly, Benjamin fumbled in his old satchel, took out some paper and started work on the fifty scientific equations he had been set for failing to do his Chemistry homework. Soon he was scribbling away furiously, for after the first couple it didn't matter if the equations didn't balance, they merely had to look good. The Chemistry master would never read them through.

The door was flung open and two fifth form boys strolled arrogantly into the form room, their new ties with the extra stripe showing they were prefects.

"There's a staff meeting this period," said the first one, whose name was Williams, "and we've come to keep you kids quiet."

Four South muttered among themselves. They knew that Williams was almost certainly lying. Fourth forms could usually be left on their own but with the headmaster's practice of making over half the fifth form into prefects, there probably weren't enough lower forms for the prefects to flex their muscles upon.

"Yes, a lot of lines," said Williams, dying to try out his new powers. The form looked at each other, then resignedly they reached for their books. Barnbrook, the First Eleven's goalkeeper, fumbled one of his textbooks, caught it, lost it and finally knocked it on to the floor. Summercourt Comprehensive was not renowned for its football prowess.

"Right," said Williams pleased. "You can write me fifty times: 'I must not make a noise in the classroom'."

"But it was an accident," protested Barnbrook.

"One hundred times."

"Oh—come on," Barnbrook said in disbelief.

"Two hundred times."

Barnbrook glared at Williams.

"And if you look at me like that again," Williams said, "I'll smack your head for you."

Four South decided to avoid trouble and the two fifth formers prowled the room, disappointed.

Hunt finally sat on the edge of Harrison's desk, inserted a finger into a hole in the brown paper cover of Harrison's textbook and tore it in a long strip.

"Look at that," Hunt said to Williams.

"Disgusting," supplied Williams. Harrison wisely didn't say anything.

"That's a valuable textbook there," said Hunt. "Make sure it gets a new cover."

Harrison nodded agreeably.

"And to make sure you do, you can show it to me tomorrow morning and I'll see it's been done really well." Harrison still failed to rise to the bait.

The two fifth formers now converged on Gaskins' desk. They stood staring at him. He shifted uneasily in his seat. Hunt put his face right up to Gaz's, Williams did the same. Gaskins flinched, then let out a snort of laughter.

"Good, I've been dying to give you some lines," said Hunt. "One hundred lines: 'The classroom is no place for demonstrations of hilarity'." He grinned at Williams.

Gaz opened his mouth, then, thinking better of it, he closed it. The two fifth formers looked around for further victims.

Benjamin finished his fiftieth equation. With a loud sigh of relief he slung his pen down, picked up his books and threw them into his desk with a bang. Then putting his feet up on the desk and leaning his chair right back, he gave out a long belch that echoed around the form room.

He groped in his blazer pocket, found an apple, took a large bite out of it and chewed it cheerfully, beaming at the two fifth formers.

Williams and Hunt gazed at him, awestruck. Everybody else was working away silently as mice, while this uncouth, ill-mannered, disrespectful prole ate apples and belched at them.

"I don't know who you are or what you're trying to prove," said Williams slowly, "but we're going to give you enough work to keep you busy for a week."

"Why don't you try detention?" Benjamin asked surprisingly.

"Eh?"

"Well you've tried lines, you've doubled them, then you've said Harrison's to re-cover his book," Benjamin continued, "the only other power you've got left is to put somebody in detention."

Williams and Hunt stared at him.

"I think that's a good idea," Williams said. "I think we'll put you in detention for a whole week."

"Only one?" Benjamin sounded surprised. He finished his apple, examined the core carefully, looked disappointed, then hurled it across the room. The prefects' eyes followed it as it curved through the air, slid down the corner of the room and fell neatly into the waste paper basket. Benjamin smiled with satisfaction.

Their eyes turned back to him.

"Two weeks," Hunt said faintly.

"Three if you like," Benjamin said readily. "It's all academic anyway."

"Eh?"

Benjamin beamed at them.

"You see—no one's going to do your lines," he said. "No one's going to go to your detentions and Harrison's not even going to cover his book." Benjamin closed his eyes and leaned back in his chair.

"If you try and disobey us," Hunt said hotly, "we'll drag you off to the Headmaster."

"Fine," Benjamin nodded. "We'll go right after the staff meeting. I could do with missing Maths anyway, I haven't done any homework again and Mr Coup is sure to be—shall we say, a trifle over-wrought?"

"We'll do just that, right after the meeting," said Hunt. Benjamin smiled happily, his eyes still closed. He could almost have been asleep, he was so relaxed.

"You don't mind going up to the Head?" demanded Williams, puzzled.

"Oh no—not in this case."

"Why not in this case?"

Benjamin sighed, opened his eyes and sat up. "I see you don't quite understand," he said easily. "You lost your power when you ripped the cover off

Harrison's book and forced Gaz to laugh so you could give him lines. You see," he continued, "if you take me to the Head, I'll tell him everything you've done in the form, and thirty-seven other people here will back me up." Benjamin beamed at them once again. "How long do you think you'll remain prefects then?"

The two fifth formers were dumbstruck. Then Williams stepped forwards, a hand raised in fury. "You little . . . I'll . . ." he froze as, to his consternation, the whole of Four South, barring Benjamin, came to their feet.

"Oh yes," Benjamin said, still meeting their gaze, "and if you lay one finger on me, we're going to punch your faces in." He closed his eyes again.

The raised hand quivered, then was reluctantly lowered. Williams would have given anything to dash it into the arrogant face that confronted him, but he didn't dare.

There was a loud tearing noise.

"Oh dear," said Benjamin, "that'll be Harrison, he must have found your briefcases." He paused, then continued in a worried voice. "He always was a little over-enthusiastic—I really don't think he's going to stop at just the covers." Benjamin yawned. "I should push off if I were you."

The two fifth formers were beaten, and they knew it. Snatching their briefcases off Harrison, who was behaving as if he were involved in a hare and hounds race, they almost ran from the room.

The form gave a cheer. Chris Jenkins turned to Benjamin.

"Quite like the old days," he said. "It's about time

we showed them that Four South's still got some teeth."

"Yes, well done Dizzy," Josey Law said loudly. Others joined in. Benjamin sat there trying not to look pleased. He turned to Rob.

"What was that you were saying about me not being one of you any more?"

7

Storm Clouds

As Morris had promised, the following Wednesday they ventured out on to the main rink to join the few other serious skaters. They were pleased to have so much ice to use but a little disconcerted by the presence of other skaters and their trainers. Occasionally the ice would be cleared while a couple went through a free programme. Both Benjamin and Belinda secretly dreaded Morris doing the same for them.

Even more off-putting was the small band of spectators that came to watch, only a few, but oh so knowledgeable.

Slowly Morris began to fit their free programme together, all the practice on the small rink beginning to pay dividends.

Although Belinda was the more accomplished ice dancer, Benjamin was in fact the better skater. Morris used his speed around the ice to good effect, even going so far as to have a professional choreographer to help work out their programme.

Meanwhile, they trained off the rink, and how they trained. They lost count of the kilometres they ran or cycled.

One Wednesday night it all came together. Skating with the music rather than to it, they completed their free programme without a single mistake. They glided to the edge of the rink where Morris was waiting.

"Well?" demanded Benjamin. "Any good?"

"Better," said Morris, "not good but better."

They grinned at each other. They knew he was pleased with them.

"We're hardly out of breath," said Belinda, "we must be getting fitter."

"Yes—I wanted a word about that," Morris said. He gestured for them to sit on one of the rinkside benches.

"Now," he said, "you train so you can skate your full programme without getting so tired that you make mistakes—right?" They nodded in unison.

"So you can never be fit enough," Morris continued, "but even knowing that, I don't want you coming off the ice looking as though it was easy."

"I don't get you," Benjamin said, puzzled.

"No, I thought that was the idea," Belinda said.

"The idea is to give your all," said Morris testily, "but you mustn't make it look easy. The one thing guaranteed to upset the judges is any show of arrogance."

"You mean you want us to look tired?" Benjamin said slowly.

"I want you to look exhausted," said Morris. "I

54

want you to come off that ice panting for breath and holding on to each other for support."

"We can do that," Benjamin said quietly.

"Good," Morris nodded. "You'll find that when it comes to the crunch you'll be out of breath anyway."

Belinda looked at him anxiously.

"Morris," she said. "We were quite good tonight, weren't we?"

"You were very good," Morris said, surprising them, "but there's still something missing."

"What?" Benjamin demanded.

"Ice dancing partners need to show a lot of emotion," Morris said, "that's what makes them so good to watch. You're still strangers out there."

There was an embarrassed silence. Benjamin and Belinda avoided each other's eyes.

"Look," said Morris, "I don't give a damn whether you hate each other's guts at school—out on that rink you've got to love each other."

Benjamin had gone bright red.

"I mean it," Morris said. "If we're going to get anywhere you're going to have to do as I say."

"I don't know how you can practise that," Belinda said in a small voice.

"Well, you'd better get it sorted out soon," said Morris. "I've entered you for a championship in seven weeks' time."

"You've what?" demanded Benjamin.

"We're not ready for it, Morris," said Belinda.

"You'll damn well have to be. You can start training four nights a week for a start."

Benjamin and Belinda were silent for a minute. Then:

"Where's it being held?" Belinda asked.

"Here, that's why you've got to enter. The rink Manager isn't going to go on letting you off your entrance money if he thinks you're not serious."

"I've never entered a championship before," Benjamin said quietly.

"Don't fuss, it's not really a championship, it's just an informal competition to encourage any new talent," Morris said. "There's no OSP, only the compulsories on the Friday night and the free dance on the Saturday."

"I'm glad to hear there's no OSP," said Benjamin. Belinda gave him a look.

"And I think there are only three judges, but don't run away with the idea that it'll be easy. There's such an interest in ice dancing they'll be coming from all over the country," Morris said. He gestured. "Let's go back to work; see if your Waltz has got any better."

They skated round almost automatically, then, when they were at the end of the rink, Belinda whispered, "You don't know what OSP stands for, do you?"

"Well, I'm sure you're going to tell me."

Belinda laughed. "Original Set Pattern," she said. "Everybody knows that."

"Course they do—it's really another compulsory, we're supplied with the tempo and we can choose the dance," she said. "Remember Torvill and Dean, when he was the matador and she was his cape?"

"Of course I do."

"That was the OSP for the eighty-three-eighty-four season."

"Good job we haven't got to do it then."

She grinned. "I don't think we're quite up to that standard just yet."

"Are you going to tell Morris that or me?"

"Can you manage four nights?" she asked.

"I haven't any choice, have I?" he said. "Oh never mind, I'll be all right."

But the following morning he wasn't so sure. When he walked into the form room Rob was waiting for him.

"We lost again last night, superstar," were Rob's first words.

"Eh—who lost what?" Benjamin asked, taken aback.

"The Under-Fifteen's—you know, your team."

"Who were you playing?"

"Don't you even know?" Rob demanded. "Rowley Regis, that's who—we hadn't lost to them for over four years."

"Oh come on," protested Benjamin. "You're not saying that if I'd been there it would have made any difference."

"Of course I am," said Rob heatedly. "We only lost by three points, someone good on the wing would have made all the difference."

"Gaz is a good winger."

"Gaz is rubbish and you know it—there isn't another man in the fourth who can run as well as you."

"Chaplin of Four North can run me off my legs," Benjamin said reasonably.

"In a straight line—yes—but that's no good." Rob's voice rose. "You've just got to play, Benjamin."

Benjamin stood very still. "I'm sorry, I can't," he said quietly.

Rob backed him against the wall.

"Now you listen to me. There's a match on Saturday and you're going to play," he said. "You've always played on the wing and I haven't anyone else who can."

Benjamin shook his head reluctantly. Rob stared at him in disbelief. Then he grabbed the lapels of Benjamin's blazer.

"You tell me what is more important than letting your best mate down?" he demanded.

"I've got to go out—I'm sorry."

"I ought to punch your head for you."

"Go ahead if you think you can, it still won't make me play." Benjamin shrugged off Rob's hands and pushed him away. Rob grabbed him again and there was a scuffle. The door opened and Mrs Hopkins walked in.

"I thought you two were supposed to be friends," she said mildly.

Rob let go of Benjamin. "So did I," he said. He went and sat down by Gaskins. Benjamin retreated to the back of the form.

Mrs Hopkins went to her desk.

"Is everybody here?" she asked shortly.

"I think so, miss," said Sally Jones, the form prefect.

"Right, mark the register please, Sally," Mrs Hopkins said. "I've got something a lot more important to discuss—I have your half-term reports here." She held up a sheaf of papers.

"Top of the form is of course Jean Wallis and just as inevitably bottom is Steven Catley." Mrs Hopkins ran her eyes down the list. "In between things are much as usual, with two notable exceptions." The form stirred uneasily. Everyone dreaded hearing his or her name.

"Firstly and most surprisingly, Belinda Thomas has dropped from sixth place to twenty-first and secondly, Benjamin has fallen from his long held position of eleventh down to thirty-third." She continued, "In addition, I have a half-page remark on each of you from the Headmaster."

Four South were silent. Benjamin wished for the end of the world.

"Right, dismiss. Belinda and Benjamin you stay behind. I want some answers from both of you."

Four South filed out, Rob without even a backward glance at his friend.

"Right you two, bring your chairs and sit here." Mrs Hopkins gestured them to her desk. Reluctantly they each dragged up a chair.

"Well?" she snapped, looking from one to the other. They were silent.

"Belinda, you I am especially disappointed with," Mrs Hopkins said. "And so is the Headmaster—to drop fifteen places in a matter of weeks is quite inexcusable."

"I'm sorry, miss,' said Belinda, inadequately.

"Don't be sorry for me," Mrs Hopkins said. "Your GCSEs are next year, you know."

"I'll put it right, miss," muttered Belinda.

"Right then—see you do. The Headmaster is talking about having your parents up to the school." Belinda was shocked into silence.

"Now run along. You'll just catch Assembly if you hurry, and shut the door after you."

Flushed and much chastened, Belinda fled the room, leaving Benjamin alone with his form mistress.

"Now then, Benjamin," said Mrs Hopkins. "I want to know what the matter is."

"I don't know what to say miss."

"That won't do," she said. "I've always treated you like an adult—now it's time to act like one."

"There just doesn't seem the time to do the work."

"That's never troubled you before." Mrs Hopkins picked up the papers and read out: "Mr Coup, Mathematics—very little homework completed this term, Mr Smythe, Chemistry—homework very badly prepared, Mrs Stars, German—no homework done at all this term—it goes on and on."

Benjamin was silent.

"Right now I'll agree with you that there are certain subjects that you virtually dropped years ago—particularly languages."

"I don't want to do languages."

"All right, I've accepted that, though heaven knows most teachers wouldn't, but only because you've been good in other subjects—Physics, Chemistry, Mathematics."

"Well, I wanted to take them at A level," Benjamin said anxiously.

"And no one up to now has doubted that you would," Mrs Hopkins said. "You're an intelligent boy but you're in danger of wasting it." Mrs

Hopkins sounded genuinely upset.

"I'm sorry miss, I haven't been thinking straight," Benjamin muttered.

Mrs Hopkins left him sitting at her desk. After a moment the door opened and Belinda came in and sat quietly opposite him.

"Was it bad?" she asked at length.

"Yes," Benjamin said miserably. "If only she had been angry, but she was . . . upset. There just doesn't seem to be enough time. I haven't told you this, but my dad's really getting at me about the skating—I told him last week about switching to ice dancing and he hit the roof."

"He thinks it's cissy, I suppose," Belinda said.

"You bet he does."

"Do you?"

"No, of course not—not now," Benjamin said. "But you can't expect everyone to understand. My dad wants me to be a rugby player, not an ice dancer."

"I can see that," Belinda said.

"Now Morris says four nights a week. I can't do the work now, what's it going to be like when we get to the competition."

Belinda was silent.

"And that business with Rob. I haven't had a fight with Rob since the second year." He looked away from Belinda. "I don't know that I can do it, Belinda."

"Perhaps if we had a word with Morris, we could miss this competition."

"Well, what are we doing it for?" Benjamin

demanded. "There's got to be one sooner or later, hasn't there?"

She nodded, "It's the same for me," she said.

"No, it's not—I'm sorry but it's not," he said. "Your parents understand, and you're not letting a rugby team down either."

"You're not letting them down."

"Of course I am. Rob hasn't got anyone else to play my position because I'd never let him drop me—I've always played."

"Rob'll get over it."

"Yes, of course he will, he always does—but it still doesn't make it right, nor does it get my school work done."

"You'll get on top of it. Surely we can work something out?"

He shook his head. "Morris warned us it meant total commitment, and look what happens. I can't even make the first hurdle."

"So what are you saying, you want to finish, is that it?"

"I don't know."

Belinda was silent for a while. Then she said, "You'll have to, if that's the way you feel about it."

"And what about you?" he demanded.

"Oh don't you worry about me," she said lightly. "I'll soon find another partner."

"I thought you said Morris had a devil of a job finding me?"

"Oh yes, then, but my old partner Steve's looking for someone again."

"Is he?"

"Yes, he rang me last week." She smiled at him wanly. "Cheer up, I'll phone Steve and we'll tell Morris tonight."

8

Last Dance

Benjamin avoided both Belinda and Rob for the rest of the morning. He felt he couldn't face the long bus journey with Belinda that night, so he left a note on her desk saying he hadn't any money and he would cycle over to the rink. Belinda searched the school for him when she found it, but he had gone home at lunchtime and didn't return for afternoon school.

That night, when he arrived at the rink, he was surprised to find her waiting in the foyer. She gave him her wan smile, then, without speaking, they went to get changed. Neither of them wanted to shock Morris by walking on to the rink in street clothes.

They needn't have worried. Morris knew something was wrong the moment they walked towards him. Their misery was obvious.

"Well!" he rapped. "What's up?"

"Benjamin has something to tell you."

"You'd better tell me then, hadn't you?" he said shortly.

Benjamin suddenly found his voice. "I've got to finish, Morris," he burst out. "I'm truly sorry but it's all getting on top of me."

Morris was silent.

"It's my school work, you see," Benjamin stammered. "I just don't have the time, what with all the training as well."

"So you're going to give up—just like that?" Morris demanded.

"I don't want to—I have to," he muttered.

"And what about Belinda? Have you thought about her—what's she going to do for a partner?"

"I'll be all right," Belinda said quickly.

"Well, then," said Morris, "and what do you plan on doing now—take your skates off and go home?"

"I suppose," muttered Benjamin.

"Even though there are people who've come specially to watch you?" Morris said.

"What people?" Belinda demanded.

"Fans, I suppose," Morris said.

"Don't be ridiculous," Benjamin snapped. "We haven't got any fans."

Morris pointed. "Well, just who the hell do you think they've come to see? Not me, and certainly not any of the other clumsy mechanics here tonight."

Benjamin and Belinda stared at the small groups of people dotted around the stands.

"Not us," said Benjamin positively.

"Oh yes, you," Morris said. "There have been more each Wednesday—you've always been too intent on your skating to notice." He glared at them

65

in disgust. "I was talking to some of them last week, one girl over there, she's about nine I think, she spends her entire pocket money travelling over from Sutton Coldfield every Wednesday—you want me to go and tell her you're not skating tonight?"

"We'll skate, Morris," Belinda said hurriedly.

"Right then." He nodded. "I'll go and put your music on, and as it's your swansong we'll do it properly. I'll clear the ice and play it over the main speakers."

"No Morris, let's just . . ."

"Just do it!" Morris interrupted. "It'll give you something to look back on." He limped away.

"Sorry," Belinda said. "What could I do?"

"That's okay," Benjamin said. "I'd like to skate with you again anyway."

Morris's voice could be heard asking for the ice to be cleared. Benjamin led Belinda on to the ice, then everything else was forgotten as their music came booming over the main speakers.

The first part of their programme went well. Benjamin and Belinda began to come alive.

They whizzed their fast section, Belinda this time matching him effortlessly for speed, then as the music changed to "Wanted" they swung into their disco sequence. This time every jump worked, every turn flowed and every lift went smoothly.

At last they were into their slow dramatic finish that left them in front of the main stands. For the first time Morris saw in their faces the emotion he had patiently been trying to instil.

The audience had risen to its feet. Even the other skaters on the side lines were applauding. Hurriedly they retreated across the ice—towards Morris.

And then they remembered. They saw the sardonic look upon his face and they remembered.

Their smiles died away and they fell silent. There was a long pause, then,

"I'm sorry Morris," said Benjamin, stepping forward. Morris regarded him in silence.

"After all your efforts," Benjamin said.

"And yours," Belinda said quickly from behind.

"Take me back," Benjamin said. "And I'll never question it again."

Suddenly Morris moved. He reached forward and grabbed Benjamin by his shirt.

"Did you feel it?" he demanded.

"What?" Benjamin flinched.

"You must have felt it." His voice rose. "I felt it once. Remember that. I was a skater too. You were born to skate; you could no more give up skating than you could breathing," he said intensely, "so don't give me your problems, I don't care about them— you're here to skate and that has got to be the most important thing in your lives or it finishes right here."

"Yes, Morris," Benjamin said quickly. Belinda nodded.

"This four nights a week, it's not enough, so forget it—I want you here five nights a week, every night but Saturday and Thursday. And Saturday mornings you're going to spend with the choreographer and when we get closer to the competition then it'll be all day Sunday as well."

"Yes Morris," Benjamin said.

"And I don't want to hear that you can't get over

on a Sunday. If you can't get a bus, then you cycle, and if you can't cycle, then you walk." Morris turned and walked away a few paces. He looked back over his shoulder. "And if you can't walk, then you crawl."

For the rest of the evening Benjamin and Belinda were very quiet. They tried to do most of their skating on the far side of the rink away from Morris. He didn't push them hard, and when the time came to finish he just nodded to them in his normal way and told them not to be late on Friday.

This time Benjamin was changed first. He waited for Belinda to appear and they walked across the car park together.

"I'm sorry, Belinda," Benjamin said. "After all the work you've put in too." She didn't answer.

"What's Steve going to say?"

"Which Steve?"

"Your ex-partner," Benjamin said. "You only phoned him tonight."

"Oh him."

"Well, won't he be put out?"

"I doubt it—he doesn't exist."

"Eh?"

"I never had a partner before you; I used to train with another girl."

"So what were you going to do?" She didn't answer. "Who were you going to skate with?"

"Perhaps I wasn't."

"I don't get you."

"Well I'd just got used to holding you upright, I didn't fancy anyone else's mistakes."

"You mean you would have given up too?"

Benjamin asked incredulously.

She shrugged, and glanced at her watch. "My bus is about to go," she said. "Goodnight Benjamin, I'll see you tomorrow."

She walked briskly away across the deserted car park.

Belinda sat on the lower deck of the bus, feeling upset at Benjamin's lack of understanding. How could he think she would go on skating if he gave up?

"Now what's that idiot trying to do?" the conductor said. Belinda jumped. Benjamin's beaming face was pressed against the bus window. It was no mean feat, since the bus was travelling at nearly thirty kilometres an hour.

A horn blared and Benjamin dropped back to let a car pass. Then, pedalling furiously, he drew level again.

She waved at him. "Go away you fool," she shouted. "You'll come a right cropper." He shook his head and nodded to the window. She knelt up and slid it open, ignoring the bus conductor's disapproving look.

"Go away," she said to the perspiring face. He shook his head again and held out his hand, she slipped her arm out and grabbed it. He gave her hand a squeeze, then at last he dropped back.

Belinda shut the window and sat down. Suddenly she felt a lot happier.

9

Perfect Partners

Benjamin was late for registration. He marched blithely into the form room and treated Mrs Hopkins to his smile.

"So glad you could make it," she said.

"Sorry I'm late, miss," he said. "I was having an argument with my dad and I had to stay to make sure I won it."

"Your father has my sympathies. Now sit down, will you please."

Benjamin glanced round the form room. Belinda wasn't there. Thoughtfully he went and sat at his desk next to Rob, who growled at him under his breath. Benjamin gave him a smile as well.

"Lend us your Maths," he said.

"What?" Rob demanded.

"Your Maths, I've got to copy it before second lesson."

Rob stared at him. "I don't believe it," he said. "You've got the cheek of the devil."

"It's all part of my charm—now hand it over, there's a good chap." Slowly Rob reached into his desk and handed Benjamin a book.

"Look," he said. "I'm trying to have a row with you."

"Yes I know, sorry I haven't got the time. Have one next week," Benjamin said cheerfully. "Look, there's no match next Saturday evening is there?"

"I'm surprised you know."

"Of course I know—I thought we could go bowling. We haven't been bowling for months."

Rob perked up immediately. "You mean you haven't got to go to the rink."

"Not Saturday evening, no."

"And you haven't got to stay in to do homework."

"Yes—but I'm not going to."

"Well, well."

"You haven't got a date then?"

"Oh yes—not with anyone special."

"You're a right charmer you are." Benjamin stood up as Mrs Hopkins left the room. "I'll see you after Assembly," he said. "I simply must do this Maths."

But Benjamin found it hard to concentrate on Rob's Maths. He sat worrying about where Belinda was. Assembly was half over before she clumped noisily into the storeroom.

She grinned her special grin.

"Hello," she said.

"Hello—you're late, did the pre's stop you?"

"Oh yes, but they never report me, I've a few friends amongst them." She smiled. Benjamin knew she meant amongst the boys not the girls.

"Where've you been?" he asked.

"Phoning Morris."

"Morris?"

"Yes, I'll explain in a minute," she said sitting down. She produced a sheaf of papers. "I've worked out a timetable for us that accommodates training, skating and homework."

"I'd like to see that." His tone belied his words.

"You will," she said. "Firstly and most importantly, Morris has agreed to us skating later each evening, seven-thirty till ten-thirty, just in time to catch the last bus home." She waved him into silence as he tried to interrupt. "If we leave home at seven that gives us one hour for tea and two hours for study."

"It takes me longer than that to have my tea," he said.

"Why?"

"I have to cook it, my dad usually works until six."

"Yes," she said. "My mum said you probably had to, so you're to have tea with us five nights a week."

"Five nights a week," protested Benjamin, "I can't let your mother cook . . ."

"You can wash up," she interrupted him. "Look, Benjamin, my parents understand it's as much for me," she said, "so accept it, will you please. I've been up all night working this out with them."

He shrugged. "Okay, we'll have to see how it goes."

"Right then, tea at my house, bring your books and your gear, then we can get two hours of homework in before we get off at seven."

Benjamin looked pained.

"Belinda," he said, "I've never done two hours homework in my life."

"It'll do you good then, won't it?" she said callously. "Next, training. What time do you get up in the morning?"

"Just after seven. I go for a run, then there's just time for some breakfast before school."

"Well, that's not too bad," she said. "From now on you get up at half-six, come round for me at seven, then we go for an hour's cycle ride."

"And when do we do our running?" Benjamin demanded. "Morris says that's as important as the cycling."

She smiled. "Lunchtimes at school, round the track."

Benjamin raised his eyebrows, then nodded. "It might work," he said.

"Course it'll work. You can get permission off Dicky Lander and no one will see us, they're not allowed round the back of the school in winter time."

"Okay then." Benjamin gave a sigh. "Let's give it a whirl."

"Right, now I must rush," she said. "I've got to catch Mrs Hopkins before she hands the register in."

Benjamin stopped her. "Do I get next Saturday night off?" he demanded.

"If you want, why?" Belinda said, thinking he was at last going to ask her out.

"I have to go bowling."

"I didn't know you liked bowling."

"I don't," he said, "but Rob does. You know he's my best friend, don't you?"

"If you say so," she said coldly.

"Well I'm trying to make sure he stays that way."

The new routine worked well for the first week. Every morning Benjamin cycled the few streets to Belinda's house, where she would be waiting, irritable and silent, as she usually was early in the day. They would go for a fast ride, always ending the hour's run with a long freewheel home when they could chatter, with Belinda by then being her cheerful self.

They would part at Belinda's house but would meet later in the storeroom, usually to work, sometimes just to talk. At lunchtime they would slip away and do some serious running around the track.

The second week though, it rained every single day. Belinda hated the rain and it took all Benjamin's powers of persuasion to get her out in the mornings. She would cycle along half-heartedly, biting Benjamin's head off every time he spoke. At lunchtime the track was a sea of mud and anyway neither of them felt like getting soaked twice in one day. When they consulted Morris, all he could do was advise them to wait, so at lunchtime they paced the school corridors like caged animals.

The rest of the routine worked better. Five nights of the week Benjamin would go to Belinda's for tea, then afterwards they would retire to the front room and work for two hours, and Belinda made sure they did work. She would stand no backsliding or idle conversation and Benjamin, whose sense of responsibility was very weak, found himself responding to her bullying.

Finally they would hurl their books away and run to catch the bus to the rink. More hours of hard work followed, using up all the energy they had left. The long bus ride home would be spent in an exhausted but friendly silence.

The competition grew nearer and nearer.

Benjamin came out of a spin, did a couple of easy steps then completed one of the finest triples he had ever managed.

"That's hardly ice dancing, is it?" Belinda said. Morris for once was late arriving. It was a Friday evening and they were on the practice rink.

"I dunno," said Benjamin. "It could be. Anyway, I don't want to forget how to do it, do I?"

"Gerrout the way then," she said charmingly. "Let's have a go."

"Watch it—you're not used to that kind of skating."

"Rats—go and teach your grandmother to suck eggs." She launched herself, skated a few quick steps and took off. She completed the first two turns perfectly but it all went wrong on the third one and she crashed into the barriers.

"Get up," said Morris, coming into the rink. Belinda climbed unsteadily to her feet and started to cry.

"You all right?" Benjamin asked.

"No."

"Serves you right for showing off," Morris snapped. She limped off the ice still sniffing. Benjamin made a move to help but Morris stopped him.

"It was the other leg," Morris said sardonically.

"Oh stuff." She stopped limping.

"You really need to hurt yourself two weeks before a competition?" he said.

"I can do a triple," she said.

"Course you can," Morris said. He turned to Benjamin and handed him the parcel he'd had under his arm. "I'm late because I had to pick these up."

"My skates?" Benjamin said, snatching the box. Belinda forgot she was hurt and excitedly the two skaters opened the box. Benjamin tried them on.

"Leave the guards on the blades till you get on the ice," Morris said. Benjamin nodded. He stepped gingerly on to the ice, then did a careful circuit of the rink.

"Well, how do they feel?" Morris asked.

"Like they're painted on," Benjamin said.

"That's what we were trying to tell you," Belinda said.

Benjamin looked embarrassed. "I want to thank both of you," he said. Belinda looked away and Morris acted though he hadn't heard.

"Do you want to try something easy first?" he asked.

"No, put the 'Wanted' tape on. Let's give them a real test run."

"If you're sure," Morris said. He sorted out the tape and Belinda joined Benjamin on the ice. This was Benjamin's favourite sequence because it was fast. This time, though, Morris could tell he was taking it easy on the turns. The music finished and they glided back across the ice to him.

"If you step off the ice without putting your

guards on I'll break your neck," Belinda said sweetly.

"Oh—right." Benjamin perched himself on the barrier.

"What's wrong with them?" Morris asked.

"Dunno—they feel a bit slippy."

Carefully Morris knelt down and examined one of the blades. He stood up.

"The groove's not deep enough for you. We can soon fix that," he said. "They just need grinding down."

"I'll get the bloke here to do them," Benjamin said.

Belinda gave a squeal of anguish. "Oh balloon brain!" she said.

Morris sighed. "If you let that butcher anywhere near those skates, Belinda won't have to break your neck—I'll do it for her."

"He does everybody else's. Isn't he any good?"

"Not for you. The tolerances you need can only be achieved by a craftsman. I'll get them done tomorrow. Now let's try a few slow steps, your compulsories need a lot of work."

The skates were better in the slower dances, giving him more confidence. Morris kept them at it for over two hours without a break before he called them back to the edge of the ice.

"How did we do, coach?" Belinda grinned.

"Well it will get better when Benjamin adjusts to his skates."

"I don't like the Waltz," Benjamin said.

"Oh, misery guts is off again," Belinda said.

"I can tell that from your skating," Morris said.

"You've got to get it right, and Belinda, you've got to learn to turn more easily."

"She turned so easily earlier on that she nearly went through the blasted ice," Benjamin said.

Morris ignored him. "You're cutting too deep edges. You shouldn't plough the ice but caress it."

"I'll see what I can do," she said sticking her elbow into Benjamin, who was laughing.

"Now, have you considered what you're going to wear?" Morris asked.

Benjamin looked stunned. "Oh no," he said. He thought for a moment. "I suppose my anorak's out of the question?"

"I think I can borrow an outfit for you," Morris said.

"I'm not going out on the ice looking like a wally."

Morris ignored him. "Now what about you, Belinda?"

"I thought I'd wear that dress I wore for my last medal," she said.

"What medal?" Benjamin demanded.

"Belinda has already taken some of the dancing medals," Morris said.

Benjamin pulled a face at her.

"You'll have to do them as well," she grinned. "Don't worry, I'll hold your hand."

"Let's leave that till after this competition," Morris said. "I think we'd better call it a night, don't you?" They both nodded. Benjamin slid the guards on to his skates, then sat on a bench to unlace them.

"Morris?" he said after a minute.

"Yes?"

"You know the night I said I'd quit?"

"Yes."

"How did you know that skating in front of an audience would change my mind for me?"

Morris gave a smile. "I was your mother's trainer," he said.

"Oh." He paused. "Why didn't you just tell me to go and get lost?"

"Usually I would have done," Morris said. "Like I told you, I don't have to run after people."

"Then why us?" Belinda asked.

"Because the lobes you cut across the ice are identical."

"The lobes—you mean the curves?" Belinda asked.

"Yes, I've never seen anything quite like it before—you see, the girl partner always cuts a smaller lobe, she has to, she's shorter. It means when the couple turn, their heads go up and down at different times. It can ruin the whole effect." Morris paused, then went on, "If you study any good ice dancers, you'll find they've adjusted to one another. It takes years of training to get it right."

"But you're saying we're already there?" Benjamin asked slowly.

"I'm saying that your lobes are matched, that's all. I found it the first night you skated together. I don't know whether it's you, Benjamin, cutting a smaller lobe, or Belinda overstretching but whatever it is, it means you're perfect partners."

On the bus on the way home, Benjamin sat silently in the corner. Belinda read her French textbook for ten minutes, then with a sigh she put it down.

"Okay, what's up?" she demanded.

"Eh?"

"You heard—something's eating you."

"I like that! It's you that's always complaining about me talking while you're studying."

"That's how I know something's up. You haven't spoken since we got on the bus."

"It's my skates."

"What's wrong with them?"

"Nothing, they're great."

"Translate that for me, will you?" she said.

"I don't want my dad to see them. He'll only ask how much they cost and then there'll be another row."

"Well, Morris has got them tonight."

"And what happens tomorrow?"

She thought for a moment. "I'll take them home with me," she said.

"That's not a bad idea—do you mind?"

"Why should I?" she said. "Then if we fall out I can always pawn them." She winked at him and went back to her book.

10

"Wanted"

Benjamin stood gazing out of the main doors at the lashing rain. It was Thursday lunchtime and their run was off again. A piercing whistle from behind made him jump.

"I've been looking for you," Rob said.

"You found me, Sherlock."

"You know this disco tonight?"

"What disco?"

"There's a school disco in the hall."

"Nobody told me." Benjamin went back to studying the rain.

"Did you have to be told?" Rob said. "I swear you live in a world of your own nowadays."

"What about it anyway?"

"Are you coming?"

"I am not," Benjamin said decidedly.

"Oh come on, don't be such a pain in the neck—you've not been out at night for months," Rob said crossly. "You're becoming a proper old woman."

"I don't dance," Benjamin said evasively. "Besides, I've got to do some work."

"Belinda Thomas is going." Benjamin felt a pang as he wondered who she was going with, then he realized he didn't really want to know.

"Oh yes," he shrugged.

Rob grinned. "Why don't you ask her?"

"Ask her what?"

"To come with you."

"Don't be ridiculous. Belinda Thomas only goes out with fifth formers, she wouldn't be seen dead with me."

"You don't know till you ask her."

"Yes I do," Benjamin said shortly.

"Well anyway you may have to come."

"Why—what do you want me for?"

"I'm going to ask Josey Law and if she tells me to take a running jump, then I can't just turn up there all on my own."

"You mean you want me as an excuse so it doesn't look like you can't pull a girl."

"You've got it—c'mon, let's go and find Josey Law."

Belinda was lying on a bench in the cloakroom with her eyes closed. Josey Law was sitting beside her having her hair done by Amanda Smith.

"How many's that you've turned down?" Belinda was saying.

"Three so far but it's hours yet till tonight," Josey said. "Who are you going with?"

"David Edison asked me twice last week," she said.

"David—what did you say?"

82

"Oh, I told him I might see him there."

"What on earth for? David's one of the few I'd accept outright."

"He's all right."

"He's gorgeous," Amanda Smith put in.

"Well who are you waiting for—Richard Gere?" Josey demanded.

"There is somebody," Belinda said, "but I don't think there's a chance in hell of him asking me."

"Who?" Josey and Amanda demanded in unison.

Belinda gave a laugh. "No chance, I'd rather announce it over the PA system than tell either of you."

Amanda stopped doing Josey's hair for a moment.

"Now what have we here?" she said. Rob and Benjamin were wandering round the cloakroom.

"Oh—it's 'Little and Large'," Josey said.

Belinda opened her eyes. "Something tells me they're coming over here," she said.

"Yours or mine?" Josey asked.

"Definitely yours—that makes four doesn't it?"

"Might be five if I can play my cards right."

"Fifty pence says you can't get Dizzy to ask you," Belinda said, shutting her eyes again.

"You're on," Josey said. She raised her voice. "Come on over, we promise not to bite."

"I'll want that in writing," Benjamin muttered to himself. Rob almost had to drag him across to the three girls.

"I've decided that I can fit you in tonight," Rob said to Josey with a grin.

"Ah—isn't that kind," she said. Amanda nodded.

"Well it's 'be kind to the under-privileged' week,"

Rob said. "What time shall I pick you up then?"

"Oh no you don't—not so fast," Josey laughed. "I haven't made my mind up—I mean Benjamin hasn't asked me yet."

Benjamin went bright red. "I'm not going," he said hastily.

"Oh, very well, I might see you there then Robert," she said. "On the other hand, David Edison's going to be there."

"Now that is taking 'be kind to the under-privileged' week too far," Rob said.

Josey laughed again. "Now push off, will you—I'm trying to have my hair done here."

This time it was Benjamin who almost dragged Rob away. Josey reached in her bag and handed Belinda fifty pence. Belinda smiled.

Benjamin stopped Rob outside the cloakroom.

"That didn't work, did it?" he demanded.

"It didn't go too badly. You've got to learn to read the situation," Rob said. "You'll have to come now, won't you?"

Benjamin gave a heavy sigh. "I'm not going to dance. I'm not going to try and pick up any girls and I'm going home early," he said resignedly.

Rob grinned. "All right, Cinderella."

By eight-thirty that night, the hall was packed with seething, shuffling, sweaty dancers. Two boys from Five East had rigged up a disco, complete with flashing lights, and were playing and re-playing the present Top Twenty.

Benjamin wasn't enjoying himself. He liked loud music as much as anyone, he even enjoyed an occasional sally around the dance floor and it amused him to see his friends all dressed up in their best clothes, pretending they weren't at school. But Belinda was there, a highly attractive and extremely well-dressed Belinda. She hadn't come with anyone apart from Josey Law, but she was dancing with every boy in sight, and most of them were fifth formers.

Benjamin glanced around. Rob had managed a couple of dances with Josey Law, but he too had eventually been ousted by the fifth formers and cutting his losses he had gone off with a plump little girl from Four North.

Benjamin decided it was time to go, the only problem being that the exit was at the other side of the cleared space they were using for a dance floor. He eased forward, ducked behind two gyrating girls and edged across the floor behind Belinda's back. Not that it mattered. She hadn't acknowledged him all evening.

He took a last look round and was just preparing to go home when contrary fate took a hand.

Somebody put on "Wanted" by the Dooleys.

Benjamin froze. This was their record.

He marched forward and tapped David Edison smartly on the shoulder. "You will excuse me," he said to the amazed fifth former. Then to Belinda, "Our dance I think."

Belinda started with surprise. She hadn't thought Benjamin had it in him. She had been watching him trying to leave for the last hour.

"Okay," she said in a neutral tone. Angrily, Edison retreated.

Benjamin couldn't disco dance very well, but he

was a superb ice dancer and he and Belinda had one big advantage—they knew each other's movements exactly and could respond to them.

So they danced. Fast, balanced steps that flowed perfectly into their next movement, in time with the music and achieving that perfection that is only reached after weeks and weeks of practice.

For the first time in his life, Benjamin was aware of people stopping to watch. A circle formed round them and they danced the short length of the record to the cheers of their classmates.

Then all too soon it was over. They finished close up, looking at each other, but without touching as they would have done on the ice. The long moment passed, then, still holding Belinda's amused gaze, Benjamin said quietly, "Thank you."

"You're off now of course." Her eyes laughed.

"I guess so."

"Goodnight then, Benjamin," she said levelly.

"Goodnight Belinda."

He turned on his heel and walked through the crowd of people. He beamed at Edison and winked at an amazed Rob as he went.

Belinda watched him, then when she was quite sure he had gone, she turned her smile on Edison who was now standing beside her.

"I'm so sorry David," she said demurely, "but I really must go home now—my parents are expecting me."

She left the disappointed Edison and walked over

to the stage where the two boys from Five East were running the disco.

"Thanks Brian," she said to one of them. "May I have my record back now?"

11

The Form Match

"I've accepted that you're not going to play any more," Rob said.

"Big of you, I'm sure."

"But you're going to play next week, aren't you?"

It was the following day and Benjamin and Rob were eating their lunch in the hall.

"I've told you I can't," Benjamin said. "Anyhow what's it matter? You've won the West Midlands Shield again—and without my help, I might add."

"You were there for most of the hard games," Rob said. "You only dropped out when the rabbits were left."

"Well then, what are you complaining about?" Benjamin swallowed a mouthful of shepherd's pie and pulled a face. "I swear school dinners get worse every day—this meat tastes like shredded dog."

"It's the form match," Rob said shortly.

"Oh."

The five fourth forms always played a knockout

match to see who would display the Shield. Fifteen boys were needed to make up each form team, which left only about four that Rob could drop.

"The school's won the Shield three times now, so we keep it," Rob said earnestly. "So if we can win the form match then its ours."

Benjamin frowned. "Well, you'll win it, won't you?" he said lamely.

"Not without you, we won't," Rob said. "Four West nearly had us last year and they've got that new chap Lurch this year."

Benjamin finished off the last of his dinner in silence.

"This match," he said. "Who arranges it?"

"Me, of course."

"Look, if you arrange it for a Thursday night I'll play—just this once."

"Consider it done," Rob said happily.

"I'm off then," Benjamin said standing up.

"Oh no—not again, where do you keep sloping off to?"

"I've got work to do."

"I don't believe you," Rob said. "You've got a bird. Only a bird would make you abandon your oldest mate."

"We're not all quite as dedicated as you," Benjamin grinned. "Anyway why don't you go and find that er—rather well-built young lady you met at the disco?"

"What, fat Valerie?" Rob said indignantly. "She should be so lucky."

"I'm sure you'll think of something to do," Benjamin laughed. "Anyway, I'm off."

Rob watched the retreating figure, wearing his most sardonic grin. "Benjamin my friend I know you too well," he said to himself. "Work my foot."

Benjamin hurried down the bank to where Belinda was already jogging around the damp track. At least it had stopped raining. It was some minutes before he could summon up the nerve to tell her about the rugby match. Her reaction took him by surprise.

"I think you should," she said.

Benjamin made a face. "What about Morris?"

"Blow Morris—he'll never know."

Rob selected a bowl, squinted down the wooden lane, took four short steps and let go. The bowl trundled up the lane and crashed into the pins. It seemed to strike dead centre but only eight went down, leaving one standing at either side.

It was Saturday evening and Benjamin and Rob were at the tenpin bowling alley in Birmingham. Benjamin wasn't doing very well.

"It's about time," Benjamin said. "Do I get a go now?"

"Not yet. You watch this." Rob's second bowl hit the left hand pin so hard that it skittered across the lane and knocked the other one over as well. "How about that then?" he exclaimed, turning to Benjamin with delight.

Benjamin wasn't watching, he was standing on one leg, trying to lift the other foot up his back to his shoulder.

"What *are* you doing?" Rob demanded.

"Eh—oh sorry." Sheepishly Benjamin lowered his foot to the floor.

"Everybody's watching. You'll get us locked up," Rob protested.

"Sorry, I was trying out a new skating move."

"I might have known," Rob sighed. He handed Benjamin a bowl. "Your turn," Benjamin sighted carefully then delivered a bowl that went into the channel.

"Does that count?" he said.

"Yes it damn well does—you've got one more go."

"I know." Benjamin selected another bowl. This time he managed to knock four of the pins over.

"Your mind's really on this," Rob said.

"I'm having an off-night, that's all."

"Mm—tell me, all this skating you do. Is it hard work?"

"Good grief, yes—a rugby match is a picnic by comparison."

"You know Belinda Thomas skates?"

"Does she? Where? I've never seen her."

"Over at Wolverhampton—Josey Law told me—you should change rinks."

"I'm happy where I am." Benjamin bowled again. Rob pretended not to notice he'd had three goes. The bowl went through the gap left by the others.

"I thought after last Thursday night you might have asked her out tonight—I could have got Josey to make up a foursome."

"Don't be daft. I happen to know she goes out every Saturday night. She'll be at some disco with that slob Edison, right now."

As Benjamin was speaking, Belinda was warming up on the practice rink. She was alone. It was five minutes before she tried her first triple of the night, only this time she didn't cry when she crashed on to the ice.

Belinda picked herself up and tried again, just as she had been doing every Saturday night for the last four weeks. Nothing was going to stop her catching up with Benjamin.

For the next few days the weather was kinder and Benjamin and Belinda were able to train every day, bringing their fitness to a peak.

Then the night of the form match brought the mildest weather for weeks. Benjamin was pleased. The ground wouldn't be too hard, so he wouldn't really risk injury. He was at home in the kitchen when the door bell rang.

"I'll get it," he called. "It'll be Rob for me." He opened the door. "You're early, I'm only—oh." Morris stood regarding him.

"What are you doing here?" Benjamin said.

"You don't seem to have a phone," Morris said.

"No. Look, come in a minute Morris, you must meet my father."

"We haven't got time," Morris said. "You both have to come to the rink with me right now."

"What, tonight?"

"Yes tonight, I'm sorry it's your night off." Morris didn't sound sorry. "Mrs Telford the choreographer's just rung me. She's going on holiday tomorrow, so tonight's the last time she can see you before the competition."

Benjamin stood frozen in disbelief.

"You know how important it is."

Benjamin nodded. "Yes of course, I'll just tell my

dad where I'm going."

Morris drove him round to fetch Belinda and waited in the car as he ran in to fetch her. Frantically, they phoned Rob but he had already left. Then they tried Chris Jenkins but there was no reply. Finally forced by Morris's impatient honking, they abandoned their attempts and rushed outside.

In the back of the car, Belinda looked as distraught as Benjamin.

"Oh Benjamin—what will they say?"

"I really don't know," he said sadly. "They haven't even got a reserve."

12

"A Damn Good Ice Dancer"

For once Benjamin was early. He could hear the noise of Four South from the end of the corridor. Resolutely he marched into the form room. A hush fell as he stepped into the ring of accusing eyes. All the boys seemed to be there and most of the girls. Belinda wasn't.

Benjamin looked for Rob. "I'm sorry Rob," he said. "I really couldn't help it." A hiss went up and grew louder. Rob was trying to shut them up.

"Who won?" Benjamin asked him.

"We lost to Four West by two points." The answer couldn't have been worse.

The form match was the only sporting occasion that drew a good amount of support. Benjamin knew the whole of Four South would have been there, bar two. Belinda wouldn't have been missed. He would have been.

"Where were you, Trueman?" Chris Jenkins' voice grated angrily.

"He was with me." Belinda's voice cut through the uproar. She stepped into the room and shut the door behind her.

"I wondered where you'd got to," Josey Law said sarcastically.

"Benjamin, I had a date last night," Rob said. "I stood her up when you asked me to play the match on a Thursday."

"We weren't on a date," Benjamin muttered.

"Well what was so important that you let the whole form down?" Chris demanded.

Belinda gave a shrug and didn't answer. If Benjamin wasn't going to tell them about the skating then she wasn't about to either. She leaned against the wall feeling angry with him. Why on earth couldn't he big enough to admit he had switched to ice dancing?

Benjamin was gazing at Belinda, hoping she would speak. When she didn't, he shook his head.

"I can't tell you where I was," he said, knowing the reaction he would get.

"Why can't you?" Barbara Wallace demanded, pushing forward. "It was a match for the Shield, you louse." She made as if to strike him.

The whole crowd surged forward and Benjamin hurriedly backed away. Belinda and Rob were shouting something but it was Chris Jenkins' massive voice that was heard.

"Leave him alone," he roared. "Let's get to the bottom of this first." Then, as the noise died down, he turned once more to Benjamin. "Are you seriously refusing to tell us why you let the form down?"

"I can't," Benjamin muttered. "I'm sorry. I just

can't . It was important, that's all I can say."

"Bull," Jeremy Reece sneered.

"You should know, that's all you ever talk," Belinda snapped. A book flew out of the crowd, just missing Benjamin. Benjamin felt afraid. He had always been one of the leading lights of Four South and to face his class mates like this was terrifying.

"Leave him alone," Chris Jenkins said. "I personally wouldn't want to soil my hands on him."

"Yes, bar him," bawled Jeremy Reece.

"Send him to Coventry," Barbara Wallace said. Everybody was agreeing with her. Benjamin felt very alone. Even Belinda seemed to have deserted him. She was leaning against the wall, studying her nails.

Abruptly, Benjamin turned and almost ran from the room.

The form subsided. Rob gave Belinda a hard look but was prevented from saying anything by the arrival of Mrs Hopkins. Reluctantly, the members of Four South dispersed to their seats. Mrs Hopkins glanced round the room.

"Where's Benjamin?" she asked.

"He's here, miss," Sally Jones supplied. Mrs Hopkins marked him present, then snapped the register shut with a bang.

"Well, I know he considers he's a law unto himself," she said crossly, "but will you kindly ask him to have the courtesy to attend registration in future?" She marched from the room.

"Mrs Hopkins," a voice called from behind her. She turned.

"Yes, Belinda." She saw with surprise that the girl was upset.

"The form just barred him," Belinda said, anger in her voice. "That's why he wasn't at registration. Benjamin wouldn't know how to be discourteous, Mrs Hopkins."

Mrs Hopkins gazed after Belinda as she disappeared up the corridor. She had just been reprimanded by one of the more respectful members of her form. She stood thinking for a moment, then gave a sigh. She went back into the form room to find Rob.

Belinda found Benjamin sitting on the bank, gazing out over the playing fields.

"Hullo," he said.

"Hullo Benjamin," she said, sitting warily on the damp grass.

"They barred me," he said as if he couldn't believe it.

"Of course they barred you," she said. "What did you expect, a nomination for sportsman of the year?"

"Thanks a bunch."

"Well you're such a fool," she snapped. "Standing there doing your strong silent act."

"Eh?"

"If you're that ashamed of being an ice dancer, then it'll never work, we'll never get anywhere—we might as well quit now, both of us."

"You're kidding."

"I'm not kidding," she said seriously. "I don't really see that there's so much difference between a free skater and an ice dancer—certainly not enough to warrant all this pretence—the way we have to ignore each other at school, the way we have to sneak off to train, and now all this."

Benjamin stared at her in disbelief.

"I'm telling you, Benjamin, it's making me sick," she said more gently. "I want to let the other girls know about you. I want to be able to go to the discos with you. I want to walk round the school with you in breaktime, the way the others do."

"Who told you I was ashamed of ice dancing?" he demanded.

"Morris of course," she said. "He didn't want you to give up. He said you'd be worried about your friends thinking it was soft."

"Well I was at first. Not nowadays though—nowadays I'm proud of being an ice-dancer—a damn good ice dancer."

She screwed up her face. "I'm missing something here," she said. "Why haven't you told anybody if you're not ashamed of it?"

"Because you didn't want anybody to know you had me for a partner of course—I was thinking of you, and look where it's got me."

"Don't talk such rubbish. What have I got to do with it?"

"Don't come Miss High-and-Mighty. *You* were the one who ignored *me*." Benjamin said. "You were always too busy going round with your posh friends, like, David Edison to want to know me at school."

Belinda closed her eyes in despair. "I haven't been out with David Edison in my life," she said. "I don't even like him very much."

"Listen, if I'd asked you to come to the disco with me, what would you have said?"

"Yes."

"You would?" he asked, astonished.

"Of course I would."

"Oh." He went down like a punctured balloon.

They sat in silence for a long while, then Benjamin said quietly, "What do you suggest I do now?"

"You could try growing a brain."

He shook his head. "Wouldn't work. You have to have something to start with."

"Well we could tell them, but I don't suppose it'll cut much ice now—will it?"

"No, they still won't understand."

"Let's win the competition, eh?" she suggested more cheerfully. "Then they will."

"We'd better damn well win after all we've been through," Benjamin said bitterly. He glanced at his watch. "First lesson's started. You'd better push off, I'll be along in a minute."

"You're not going to cut it, are you?" she demanded, getting to her feet.

"No, I've got to face them sometime," he said. He watched as Belinda reluctantly left him sitting there. He gave a sigh; at least he could try and keep her out of trouble with the form.

The lesson had started when Benjamin knocked respectfully and entered.

"Come along now, Benjamin," Mrs Hopkins said shortly. "You're already ten minutes late."

"Sorry miss." He walked to his accustomed seat at the back and sat down.

Rob sat transfixed, then inexorably the whole of Four South turned to look at him. He bent his head as he slid his books into his briefcase. "I'm sorry," he

whispered, without moving his lips, "I have to or they'll bar me too."

"Yes of course I understand," Benjamin murmured, "don't worry about it."

Rob stood up, walked forward and plonked himself down by Harrison, two rows ahead. For the first time in his life, Benjamin found himself sitting alone. It wasn't a nice feeling.

The form sat in silence. Mrs Hopkins was writing on the board, pretending she hadn't seen the little drama that had just been enacted.

A chair grated and Four South stared in amazement as Belinda Thomas stood up. She said something quietly to Josey Law then, smiling brightly, she walked across and sat down in Rob's seat alongside Benjamin.

For the first time in the history of Four South a girl and boy had chosen to sit together. In disbelief, the form strained its ears to hear what they would say to one another. The form was disappointed.

"I hope you did the homework," Benjamin said offhandedly.

"You're kidding. I'm copying off you," Belinda replied.

Rob was smiling his sardonic smile again.

13

The Compulsories

"I can't understand why they haven't barred you," Benjamin said. They were sitting in the storeroom during Wednesday's Assembly.

"Oh I knew they wouldn't," Belinda said. "The girls are not quite as autocratic as the boys you know."

"They've sent me to Coventry," he said, aggrieved.

"Of course they have. They're still very cross with you," she said. "But they're coming round slowly."

"I hope so, I mean it's not so bad when you're there but in the subjects you don't take, it's a bit lonely."

"You know Rob had a fight with Reegie?" she said.

"Yes. Don't tell anybody but Rob was round my house Saturday evening."

"Do you know what it was about?"

"He wouldn't say, but it was obviously about

me—Reegie probably shot his mouth off."

"Actually, he said something about me," she said deflating him. "He said I should be barred as well."

"Oh." Benjamin looked put out. "Anyway you have to punch Reegie's head occasionally. I've been doing it for years."

"Well, you're not to do it this week, not till after Saturday," she said. "I wouldn't worry about it anyway. Nobody ever takes any notice of Reegie. In fact I think the form's getting fed up with this whole business."

"You think they might start talking to me again soon, do you?"

She pulled a face. "They might have done," she said. "But there's something I haven't told you."

"Go on—it couldn't be anything worse."

"Rob's found out it's Mrs Hopkins' thirtieth birthday," she said, "and he wants the whole form to take her out to celebrate."

"Rob does?" Benjamin was surprised. "Bit soft for Four South isn't it?"

"Come on, Benjamin, we owe her a lot—she's the best teacher this school's got."

"I agree with you. I think it's a nice gesture," Benjamin said.

"Well they wanted you to come too—and me of course. I told them no."

"Why?" protested Benjamin. "It's just the opening we're looking for, and even Morris would let us fit that in."

"It's the night of the competition."

"Oh."

"Yes and I'm afraid you can't alter birthdays."

"I don't know about you—I'll be glad when Saturday's over," he said.

"And Friday. Don't forget the compulsories. You're going to show off your Waltz."

"Don't remind me—we'd better run through the whole programme with Morris tonight."

"Yes, but he won't work us too hard tonight."

"Won't he? Good grief." Benjamin looked stunned.

"No, and he wants us to have a break from training all Thursday."

"I won't know what to do with myself, all that free time," Benjamin thought for a moment. "Tell you what. Do you want to go out?"

Belinda blinked. After all this time, he'd finally asked her for a date, and it had to be just before the competition.

"What do you suggest?" she said in a neutral voice.

"How about a disco, or a film if you prefer."

"Don't think I could concentrate, could you?"

He shook his head. "I suppose not."

"We'll go out next week to celebrate."

"If we win," Benjamin said.

"Or if we lose. At least it'll be over. Still leaves tomorrow night, doesn't it?"

"Yes." He thought for a moment, then brightened. "I know. Let's go for a training ride."

Belinda started to laugh.

There was no game on Thursday night, so Rob and Chris Jenkins were having yet another attempt at Paul Hill. Paul Hill is the steepest hill in the Midlands; it goes upwards with an ever increasing gradient for over a kilometre.

Rob's breath was coming out in long drawn out shudders. Behind him he could hear Chris Jenkins puffing away like a beached whale. Rob wobbled, nearly gave up, then with an effort he forced his bike straight and stamped hard on the pedals with his last reserves of strength.

His knees felt as if they were screaming, his thigh muscles were tightening, and his lungs were on fire. Rob risked a glance forwards—the hill glowered unmercifully back at him, half its length still to go. It finished him. He let his bike fall with a crash and slumped on one of the many stone seats that an understanding county council had considerately dotted the length of the hill.

Chris Jenkins had dismounted some eighteen metres back and slowly he made his way up to where Rob was sitting.

"I don't believe it," Chris gasped. "No one could ride up this." Rob couldn't answer.

The two boys sat quietly as their lungs slowly came back under control.

"Stop relying on your gears," came a voice. Rob sat up, he knew that voice.

"And sit down," the voice added severely.

"Rats—go and teach your grandmother to suck eggs," came the caustic reply.

The two boys stared as Benjamin shot past on his bike, Belinda close behind. Not seeing Chris or Rob in their concentration they threw themselves at the massive hill.

Without a word the two boys grabbed their bikes and marched as fast as they could after them. Once more breathing heavily they staggered over the brow of the hill, some five minutes after Benjamin and Belinda had disappeared from view.

Silently they gazed out over the two kilometre long stretch of road they could see from the top. There was no one in sight.

"Well, I suppose we should be getting back," Chris said unhappily.

"Yes, I suppose so." Rob threw his leg over his machine and turned it around to roll back down the hill. "Chris," he said quietly.

"What?"

"That old bike of Benjamin's."

"What about it?"

"It hasn't got any gears." Rob released his brakes and hurtled off down the long hill.

At long last Friday night arrived. Benjamin and Belinda hardly said a word on the bus, all the way to the rink. Seven-thirty found them sitting in a huddle with Morris.

"Have they all come?" Benjamin asked Morris. He was still amazed at the number of couples that had entered.

"Yes. Forty-one couples out of the forty-two that entered have arrived. Jenny Strick from Sheffield had a very bad fall earlier in the week."

"There but for the grace of God," Belinda muttered.

"And only twelve go through?" Benjamin asked for the umpteenth time.

"Just go out and skate normally. Don't try and be

clever and you'll do fine. You'll get through to tomorrow."

"I hate the Waltz," Benjamin muttered.

"As long as you don't let it show—it's only one of the three anyway—you can let yourselves go tomorrow."

"Why does everybody else look so blasted confident?" demanded Benjamin.

"They're feeling just the same as you," Morris assured him.

"They couldn't be," Benjamin muttered.

"I was listening to some of the other girls in the changing rooms," Belinda said. "They've been entering these competitions for years."

"Entering them, yes," Morris said. "I bet none of them mentioned winning, did they?"

"Well none that I heard," she admitted.

"Well then—look—they wouldn't even be entering for a minor competition like this if they'd ever won anything," Morris said. "Don't be in awe of this lot."

"Right Morris." Benjamin sounded unconvinced. The compère's voice was calling for the first couple. Benjamin and Belinda were skating nineteenth.

"Well, we'd better go and watch," Belinda said uncertainly.

"I wouldn't advise it," Morris said.

"We can't just sit here," Benjamin protested. "Anyway, I want to see just what we're up against."

"It's your decision," Morris said reasonably, "but I'm still advising you against it." Benjamin looked at Belinda, who gave a nod.

"I want to watch it," Benjamin said. "Just this once."

Benjamin and Belinda sat alongside Morris in the nearly empty stands. Nobody ever came to watch the qualifying rounds. The first few couples ventured on to the ice and danced the required steps with capability if not enthusiasm. After the fifth couple had skated Benjamin turned to Morris.

"We're better than this," he said quietly.

"I told you that you were," he said, "but don't underestimate them. There are some good working skaters here. None of them will ever win anything major but most of them will go through to the final."

Slowly their turn came round and their stomachs grew more and more knotted. Then when they were called it was almost an anti-climax as they stepped on to the ice.

Suddenly the music started and their nerves faded as they swung into their routine. They flew around the ice using the whole rink, not staying nervously in the middle like many of the others. Their confidence soared and they began to go even faster. The steps had to be repeated over and over again, but even so there was plenty of room to show their superiority. It was all so easy after the discipline of Morris's training that by just a fraction, they began to show off and their moves became more flamboyant. On the third and final circuit of the rink Benjamin spun Belinda round and when he reached out for the solid contact of her hand it wasn't there.

Their fingertips just brushed and Belinda spun over and crashed on to the ice.

"At least you got up straight away," Benjamin said. "We managed to finish anyway."

"Finish is the right word," said Belinda.

They were sitting miserably in the back of the rink, hiding from everybody.

"It was my fault," Benjamin said soberly.

She shook her head. "It was both our faults," she said. "Morris warned us about being arrogant and the very first time . . ." She broke off and looked as if she were about cry.

"There'll be another time."

"No there won't. Morris won't waste any more of his training on us."

"We'll let me decide that," Morris said from behind them. They both jumped.

"Morris, we're so very sorry," Benjamin said earnestly.

"You certainly ought to be," he said. "You're the only ones that fell—did you know that?" They both avoided his gaze.

"There's not another couple out there that can come anywhere near you," Morris went on, "but you had to go and watch and find that out—that's why you fell. Big-headedness, that's all—sheer big-headedness."

"We know," Benjamin said coming to his feet, "and we're sorry. Now can we leave it alone, Morris? I've had enough for tonight."

"Okay, go and get changed," Morris said, "and I'll see you here tomorrow night."

"Here?" Belinda asked. "You surely don't want us to come and watch, do you?"

"I certainly don't."

"Then what are you on about?" Benjamin demanded.

Morris gave a smile. "Didn't I tell you?" he said. "You were placed seventh."

14

The Ice Mountain

Belinda brought her skate bag round in an arc that connected beautifully with the side of Benjamin's head.

"Ow, what was that for?" he demanded. It was Saturday night and they were threading their way between the cars in the packed car park of the rink.

"I'm showing you that I've remembered my skates," she said. "After all, that was the fourth time you'd asked me tonight—anybody would think you were nervous."

"Too right I am. Never mind the competition, I've got to wear this monkey suit!"

Benjamin had worn a skating outfit he'd had for years for the compulsories, but Morris had produced a modern one for the final. He'd insisted that they wore different outfits for each night.

They went in through the back entrance of the rink and disappeared to their respective changing rooms. Benjamin stood self-consciously in the corridor waiting for Belinda but when she came out, she looked so different that at first he didn't recognize her, that was, until she opened her mouth.

"Ooo, it's a penguin," she said eyeing him up and down.

"That does it, I'm off home," he said. She walked round him, studying him as though he were a horse.

"You'll do," she said grudgingly, "only I wouldn't bend over in those trousers if I were you."

"I was going to tell you how nice you looked, but I don't think I'll bother now."

"That's all right. Someone's bound to tell me," she said.

"I don't suppose for one moment anyone will notice," he said. "C'mon, let's go and see if Morris has bothered to turn up."

Morris seemed to be the only relaxed person there. He waved to them as they wandered into the ante-room.

"You look marvellous, Belinda," were his first words.

"Oh, stuff," said Benjamin. Belinda grinned at him.

"You look pretty smart too," Morris added, to Benjamin.

"Pretty is the word," Belinda said.

"I have it on the best authority that I look like a penguin," Benjamin said.

"Don't worry about him, Morris, he'll listen to anybody," she said. "Do you know what position we are skating yet?"

"Last," Morris said.

"Great," Belinda said. "Couldn't be better."

"It's a bit of a wait from the warm up isn't it?" Benjamin asked.

"Going last means that the judges can compare your performance against the entire field," Morris said. "Most skaters would give their eye-teeth for the last place."

"I guess," Benjamin nodded. "Are there many people out there watching?"

Morris sighed. "It's packed," he said. "Why on earth did you think I said I would keep seats for your dad and Belinda's parents?"

Belinda saw Benjamin's face fall. "Hasn't he come?" she asked.

"You're kidding."

"Oh, I'm sorry, Benjamin," Belinda said putting her hand sympathetically on his arm.

"Listen, he wished me luck, so I figure I'm ahead of the game with that."

"I've just been talking to your parents, Belinda," Morris said. "They're in the front row."

"Well how did they get here?" Benjamin asked in a puzzled voice.

"They got a lift," Belinda said.

"Why didn't you come with them?"

She avoided his eyes. "Oh, I dunno—I suppose I wanted to make sure that you didn't chicken out on me."

"Well I'm going out to watch," Morris said. "Look, don't you go expecting any magnificent scores, not at this level, three is respectable, anything above—good."

"What are you going to do?" Benjamin asked.

"We are staying right here," Belinda said sternly.

112

"I've got some homework to do and so, incidentally, have you."

"You're having me on," Benjamin said.

"I'm not. Life goes on after the competition you know," she said. "Anyway I'm not going to sit here brooding."

Morris laughed callously. "Good idea," he said. "I'll let you know what's happening."

Five minutes later the skaters all warmed up together. Then the ice was cleared and Benjamin and Belinda retreated behind the screen. Then came the bustle of the final seats being filled before the compère's voice announced the first couple. Benjamin dragged his mind away from the music and tried unsuccessfully to join Belinda in some work. She wasn't getting much done either.

The minutes passed. Each one seemed an hour. Slowly, remorselessly, their turn drew nearer. Morris appeared, making them both jump.

"That's number ten," he said, "not long now." Then he was gone before they could question him. Belinda packed away her books and they checked their skates for the hundredth time.

Number eleven was announced and suddenly they were next. In silence they sat listening to the music playing away their last few minutes. Benjamin looked at Belinda. He suddenly realized that she was terrified. It was the first time he had seen her disconcerted.

"Don't worry," he said reassuringly, "we'll knock 'em dead." She gave a wan smile. "I meant to tell you," he added, "you're looking really great tonight." This time she gave her normal grin.

The music of the last couple faded. Benjamin took Belinda firmly by the hand and led her towards the entrance. Morris waved them on. "Don't know the exact points," he said, "but fours will give it to you."

The compère's voice was saying, "And from the home rink . . ."

"Stay on your feet," from Morris.

"Belinda Thomas and Benjamin Trueman." They skated forward into the mass of light. And then the adrenalin flowed, their self-consciousness died, their reserve faded. They swished easily into the centre of the rink, remembered to acknowledge the judges, then took up their stance.

Their music surged out and lifted them effort-lessly with it. Every step was performed with a flowing accuracy that left the audience silent with admiration. The first part of the routine flashed by and they were enjoying it as much as the spectators; the music so unusually loud over the main speakers; the massive feeling of the packed stands; the clinical eyes of the judges.

They reached the middle of the programme and the music changed to "Wanted", the record that Benjamin had insisted on keeping in. This was the bit that the audience would really understand as their steps became much faster and more modern. Then the music changed again, for the last time, and their skating took on a more classical beauty before the music finally died away, leaving them frozen in a single spotlight.

The crowd went wild, especially their own loyal group of fans. Their nervousness returned with a bang and they almost ran back across the ice to where Morris was waiting.

Morris was bawling over the row to them. He gave Benjamin a hug and kissed Belinda. They were both panting for breath, just as Morris said they would, both of them laughing with the joy of the moment.

A hush fell, then the biggest roar yet as their first set of marks went up:

4.5, 4.0, 4.5.

Belinda was crying with emotion. Benjamin nearly was too. The second marks went up:

4.5, 4.5, 4.5.

The crowd voiced their approval.

"That's good enough!" Morris shouted. "I knew you'd do it."

They sat drinking in the occasion, then Morris took them down the passage, away from the uproar. He left them with the other skaters and returned to the rink.

"Was it worth it?" Belinda asked Benjamin happily.

"Oh yes, it was worth it," he gasped. They stood quietly, getting their breath back, then Benjamin whispered to her, "We did win, didn't we?"

"I don't know, but the crowd thinks we have anyway." She gave him a wink.

"Can't you tell from the points?" he demanded. "You've seen these things before—you told me you have."

"I never said I understood the marking, did I? It's ever so complicated," she said. "You're better at Maths than me, you can handle it for the next one."

"The next one?"

"Well there is going to be a next one, isn't there?"

She gazed anxiously at him.

He smiled into her eyes. "You just try and stop me."

At last the judges worked out the points and the skaters were called in reverse order, the other couples trying to look pleased. And only when their names were called did they really believe they'd done it. Then they were stepping up on to the central position of a podium that had appeared on the ice and the crowd were letting the judges know that they had made the right decision.

The rink Manager, dressed in bow tie, dinner jacket and skates came forward, shook each of the boys' hands, kissed each of the girls and hung a ribbon round their necks. A boy glided up and handed a microphone to him. He waved to the skaters to stay where they were and waited as the crowd fell silent.

"Ladies and Gentlemen," he began, "I think you will all agree that we have been privileged to see some marvellous skating here tonight." He had to wait for the crowd to quieten again. "I think it's very encouraging to see so much talent and enthusiasm from our young skaters," he continued. "Now I know I shouldn't pick any of them out especially, but I really must mention the two I know from the home rink, Belinda Thomas and Benjamin Trueman."

Benjamin jumped at his name, he hadn't realized anyone had noticed him before.

"They have been here five nights a week every week without pause for months. Where they get the energy from I do not pretend to know, but they've realized there is no other route to the top. The days of the part-time athlete have gone for ever. Only by the most fiendish dedication can any young sportsman or woman hope to compete with any measure of success." He paused for breath, then, "I have seen them doing the same steps, the same movements, again and again until they have virtually wept with frustration. I have seen them take falls that would prostrate a normal person, and be up and skating within seconds, and I have seen them so weary at the end of a practice that they can hardly walk up the stairs off the rink."

Benjamin risked a glance at Belinda. She had gone bright red.

"And I know that when we are in bed, or sitting watching television, or out enjoying ourselves, that all these young men and women are out training—every moment they can spare.

"But for what a result. I think everyone here tonight will agree that we have witnessed the debut of two future stars. Everything they have given up, their friends and their social life—all the work they have put in, the hours of practice, the weeks of training, have finally reaped their reward." The Manager finally paused for breath. "Ladies and Gentlemen, I ask you once again for your applause for the winners here tonight—Belinda Thomas and Benjamin Trueman."

The crowd rose again.

"I only wish Four South could have heard that!" Benjamin shouted to Belinda over the din.

"They did!" she bawled back.

"What?"

"They did." She pointed. "They're all in the front

117

row, over there—the ones standing on the seats."
She laughed.

Benjamin stared. Then, "You arranged this—you
and Rob."

"Mainly Rob." She was only half talking to him,
busy waving round the rink. "He guessed a while
ago," she said. "So we arranged to bring Mrs
Hopkins here tonight. She said she liked ice dancing,
if you remember?"

Benjamin was feeling his life sliding back into
place once more. He gave up trying to speak over the
noise. Belinda had put an arm unashamedly round
him.

Together they were climbing the Ice Mountain.

Some other Hippo Books to look out for:

THE LITTLE GYMNAST
Sheila Haigh

0 590 70407 7 £1.25

Anda has a natural talent for gymnastics and makes startling progress at the Ferndale Olympic Gymnastics Club. But Anda's parents are poor and gymnastics is an expensive hobby.

Will Anda have to give up her hopes of becoming an Olympic Champion?

SOMERSAULTS
Sheila Haigh

0 590 70787 6 £1.50 (published February 1988)

Anda Barnes has won a six-week scholarship to train at a top London gym club! That *proves* that Anda is good! But life at the club comes as quite a shock — everyone else is so good. They perform complicated manoeuvres with apparent ease, and Anda can do nothing right now that she's here, no matter how hard she trains.

Has Anda really got what it takes to become a champion?

SNOOKERED
Michael Hardcastle

0 590 70906 2 £1.50   (published March 1988)

What happens when you're a talented young snooker player with nowhere to play? Kevin Ashburn's struggle for recognition is tough, but can a chance meeting with a snooker professional give Kevin his lucky break?